The Disruptor

by

Ray Sherry

Copyright 2019 GreenForce (Wales) Limited)

The right of Ray Sherry to be identified as the Author of the Work has been asserted by him in accordance with the Copyright, Designs and Patents Act 1988.

First Published in 2019

by GreenForce (Wales) Limited

Apart for any permitted use under UK copyright law, this publication may only be reproduced, stored, or transmitted, in any form, or by any means, with prior permission in writing of the publisher or, or in the case of reprographic production, in accordance with the terms and the licenses issued by the Copyright Licensing Agency.

All characters in this publication are fictitious and any resemblance to real persons, living or dead, is purely coincidental.

ISBN 978-1-9160639-1-4

Dedication

to

everyone and anyone striving

to bring their ideas for innovation and

disruption

to the global market place

for the greater good of mankind.

Preface

The World is changing faster than at any time in history. In the past fifteen years, technological innovation has advanced more than in the previous two thousand years combined. The use of technology is everywhere. Modern life as we know it, could not exist today without technology.

The world population currently stands at over seven billion people. Feeding such numbers relies heavily on the use of the latest technology; from the farmer in the field, with his highly advanced GPS guided combine harvester, to the supermarket checkout that uses barcode scanning equipment; all is made possible through recent advances in technology.

Beyond the canon ball and musket, our countries have, for many years, been defended by technology; every naval ship, military utility vehicle, guided missile, light armament and now drones, are driven by technology.

Even the mass-produced synthetic clothes we wear and the gluten free food we eat are made possible through technology. Cars, aeroplanes, trains and all other forms of transport, have been mass produced using technology, which is also extensively incorporated into dashboards, warning systems, monitoring systems and navigation systems.

Look around your kitchen and count how many items have an onboard microprocessor and then count the items that could not have been manufactured without the use of technology. Ninety-nine per cent of what we produce today is technology dependent – the fresh food in the refrigerator has probably been harvested using some form of technology, sorted and packaged by technology and distributed by a vehicle using technology. Even the refrigerator used to store the food is driven by technology.

Let's face it, the Industrial Revolution was just the tip of the iceberg. Who would have thought that just one hundred and fifty years later, this revolution and its attendant massive increase in the burning of fossil fuels would be regarded as the catalyst behind global warming? And yet mankind is on the cutting edge of the greatest period of technological advancement never imagined by even the greatest of innovators and scientists.

What makes this all scary., is that the world is truly only a few years, in relative terms, into the 4th Industrial Revolution – The Digital Revolution! The Internet of Things (IoT), Artificial Intelligence (AI), Advanced Humanoid Robotics, Natural Language Processing (NLP), Drone Technology and many more, and whilst having been in use for some time, are only just emerging into the mainstream. And Distributed Ledger Technology (DLT) might just be biggest disruptor of all if only the masses could grasp its potential.

As humans, we find it hard to put our phones aside for a few moments to concentrate on the real world. Our heads are constantly down, scanning social media for news of something or nothing. Modern technology is critical to our way of life, but our way of life, our way of living, is also under threat because of our abuse of that same technology.

The Disruptor considers technology in a powerful and highly beneficial way! It takes disruption to a new level, but unlike the Millennium Bug, which had hundreds of millions spent on it, with virtually no benefits to the consumer, the disruptive idea in this book would cost less than £50,000 and be very consumer friendly. Everyone of one us could potentially save hundreds, if not thousands of pounds every year, make the world a safer place and reduce the impact on the planet.

If we harness technology in the right way, then its use could help protect our way of life as well as enhance it for future generations to come.

Before the Disruption

Chapter 1

Marku Sala unfastened his seat belt and retrieved his bag from the overhead storage. He was hemmed in by other passengers, in front and behind, so couldn't go anywhere. The captain announced the arrival of the air bridge, and that it would only be a few minutes to disembarkation. The young Romanian drew a deep breath, sensing the aircraft's front door had been opened. He could feel the cool morning air circle around his feet. Up ahead, he could see people lifting their own bags from the overhead rack. It was the sign. He would soon be off the plane and once on British territory, he could begin his new adventure.

He remembered his final argument with *The Wolf* and saying good-bye to his older sister, Anna which was such a bitter sweet moment. He'd been an active cybercriminal since entering his teens, and quickly became a highly regarded talent in the dark web community. But his regular disagreements with *The Wolf* had become more and more unsavoury. He decided to quit and look for a job as an ethical hacker in London. Anna was happy for him. She too was trying to break away from that life but stayed behind to try and convince *The Wolf* to do the same – to give it all up and move to the UK. *The Wolf* wasn't so easily persuaded.

The passengers in front began to move. Stepping off the aircraft, Marku's excitement rose. He'd made the decision to leave late the night before and had only packed a small bag. Arriving in a new country for the first time, this bag was all he had.

'I don't need much,' he assured himself, 'just my passport, cards, cash, a few toiletries and a change of clothes.' He would enjoy his first shopping experience later, once he'd checked into his hotel. He smiled and felt good about his decision.

At immigration, he queued with all the other passengers who didn't hold e-passports. The queue moved quickly and soon he was standing at the yellow line, the next to be scrutinised by an immigration officer. A booth number was called, and Marku stepped forward, handing his passport to the waiting officer. It seemed to take an age. The official was looking closely at his passport photograph whilst tapping buttons on his computer screen.
'The purpose of your visit?' enquired the immigration officer.
Marku replied, being slightly economical with the truth.
'I've got a new job here in London'.
'What do you do?'
'I'm a computer specialist.'
'What type of computer specialist?'
'I'm a White Hat, an ethical hacker,' replied Marku, proudly.
'A White Hat, you say? Hmmm, that sounds interesting. So interesting that my two colleagues

here would like to have a longer conversation with you.'

Marku's passport was given to one of the awaiting officers now standing behind him. He felt uneasy, so turned to face them.

'Please come this way sir. We'd like to ask you a few questions.'

The first immigration officer waved them away and pressed his *available* button for the booth, ready to scrutinise the passport details of the next visitor.

Marku Sala was taken to an interview room and eventually charged by the police with cybercrimes against the United Kingdom. He refused the offer of a phone call, preferring instead to keep Anna out of things and as far away from trouble as was possible.

After due process, Marku's case didn't reach court. The powers that be had other plans for a man with his valuable skillset. Instead, he was persuaded to cooperate with the authorities and take a different job working for the intelligence services at the Cybercrime Unit at New Scotland Yard. It wasn't the job he had been expecting, but it did keep him out of prison and most attractively, the salary was better. He was starting his new adventure after all, but under the new name of Adam Barth. By stipulation, he was now under the strict control of the UK Intelligence Services and had to forget his past. The hardest part was that he would never see his sister, Anna, again.

Chapter 2

'Sexy tech! No techie sex! Noooo!' screamed Michael Day as he hurriedly tried to find a gripping punch line to end his final year essay.

'Why not geek? Geeky geek?' retorted Leonard Tall.

'Get lost Tall. Go pick on someone who gives a shit!'

The final year *A-level* students continued to spar until neither gave the other a second thought. Tall was a bully and made Michael's school life a daily challenge.

Mike shrugged off his thoughts and continued talking with Lisa, his wife, whilst reading the morning news on his tablet.

'You know darling, I have no idea why I keep getting these flashbacks. It's been years since I had a momentary thought about that arsehole, Lenny Tall, but here I am, thirty-odd years later and still getting reminders of those days - I just don't understand it?'

'Sounds like you're stressing over it. Do you think Leonard what's his name is haunting you?'

'Maybe? Nah! I was just watching TechWatch last night, and I can't help feeling that something's afoot. No idea what, though! Last time I saw him was the day we left school after our *A-Level* results and he was being his usual arrogant, annoying self. Even the odd time when I've seen him on television, like last night, I don't give him a second thought.

Hitting the mute button on the remote control when he speaks is good fun though.' Mike laughed.
'Darling, if you ask me...'
'Which I'm not,' said Mike, jumping in.
'He is haunting you,' continued Lisa, undaunted.
'And you don't know what to do about it! Ironic really, you being the problem solver in the family,' she laughed. Mike didn't.
'It says here, that **Radio Shack has gone bust.**'
'Radio Shack? What do they do?' quizzed Lisa.

Mike read aloud.

'Radio Shack reigned supreme in the electronics in the pre-internet days, but the company failed to successfully adapt its business model and faced a fate like much of the rest of the retail electronics industry. With products easily being sold through online channels, traditional brick-and-mortar, electronics retailers have been among the most vulnerable to the growth of Amazon.'

'Wow! That's a surprise. Didn't you buy something from them last year?' asked Lisa.
Mike continued to read.
'It goes on to say that the company has declared bankruptcy, following a prior bankruptcy filing in 2015. By the end of May the company says it would have closed 1,000 stores, with just 70 company-owned stores remaining open, along with 460 dealer-owned stores. While the brand still exists today, it's a mere shell of its former self.'

'Interesting.' Acknowledged Lisa, but she was far more interested in her latest innovation hot from the oven, than the latest disruptive news hot off the press.

'As I've always said with the increased use of the internet and the buying power of companies like Amazon, it's only a matter of time before they take business away from the traditional high street and the out of town retail parks. Part of the problem is that companies like Radio Shack see the impact coming but they just can't change quick enough. And then it's too late.'

'What do you think?' Lisa interrupted.

'I've just told you what I think,' retorted Mike.

'No, not the damned internet. What do you think of my latest creation - my cake?'

'Looks like a large brick from the Victorian era. What's that hole in the middle?'

'That, my dear Michael, is art,' she sighed.

'Looks like burnt art to me.'

'I think we need a new oven. I just can't get the temperature or the cooking time right these days.'

'Maybe I should get a new techie sexy wife – one that knows how to bake a simple cake? Not a brick!' They both laughed.

Like Radio Shack, the causalities of the internet and smartphone revolution were ever increasing. Mike continued reading, taking note that Toys R Us had ceased trading and had gone into administration, as had British Home Stores the year before, affecting some 11,000 employees and closing over 160 stores.

In his professional capacity, Michael Day, professionally Mike Day, was something of a technology renegade and was increasingly being regarded as a digital disruptor. His services extended to advising industry and corporate entities on the potential opportunities and threats of digital technology. He'd learned that when digital technology was applied in a specific way, it had the potential to disrupt any industry. He would regularly present at conferences and was eagerly awaiting the UK Insurance Industry annual conference at which he was due to speak.

While Lisa pondered over her latest failure, Mike put down his smart tablet and continued work on his latest conference presentation. There were just a few final edits to apply. Since adopting the title *Digital Disruptor,* he'd been presenting up and down the country and was breaking into the international circuit as well. Style-wise, he preferred to just speak with the odd visual prompt, ideally interactively, with the audience. More typically he found that conference organisers decided the rules and a more comprehensive set of slides was the accepted norm, much to his disliking. He momentarily recalled the words in the speaker briefing notes.

'And each presentation must have a minimum of twenty slides, or else!'

He chuckled inside.

'Or else my speech will be a disaster and I'll never be able to show my face around these parts ever again?' he chuckled again. 'Or else someone will cry; or else the world would end in an instant.'

Eventually running out of *or elses*, he returned to what he was doing.

Over the past five years, Mike had amassed a huge library of tech-related case studies, artefacts, market data, customer success stories and, of course, the inevitable failures. Case studies were his favourites, especially those involving a human element with amazing, if not unsustainable, service.

He thought back to a story he'd read about two years earlier when a train passenger sent a message to the train operator via social media to say he couldn't vacate the toilet because there was no toilet paper. The train operator's social media administrator saw the message, contacted the train driver who then passed the message on to the guard. Within ten minutes, there was a knock at the toilet door and the paper was delivered. The guard never did find out who the person was he helped that day, but the rail operator got a lot of positive feedback from the public. The guard and the social media administrator received a customer service award and £100 each.

After completing his twenty-one-slide presentation, Mike dug a bit deeper into his archives. Flicking through, he smiled when he saw one of his all-time favourites. He read it quietly to himself.

It was about a little girl who somehow managed to post on a popular social media site that she was watching mummy sleeping on the floor. In fact, mummy had fallen and lay unconscious. The post was seen by a member of the family who reckoned it was a bit odd. After a quick trip across town, the family member entered the house only to find their relative, unconscious on the kitchen floor. An ambulance was called and within twenty-minutes, the child's mummy was conscious again on her way to hospital. Thankfully, she made a full recovery but did have a sore head for days afterwards. The little girl was treated to her favourite pizza and allowed to stay up later than normal that night for being so good. The story went viral and was viewed by over 45 million people.

Mike smiled and continued reading through his archives. He came across some old statistics that, in their day, were truly unbelievable.

'Darling listen to this,' he called out and began reading another article.

'How the world is changing! Radio, for example, took 38 years to reach 50 million listeners but in 2012, when one of the main search engines launched an electronic wallet, it took just three days to reach the same audience number. That's mind-blowing, don't you think? he asked out loud.

'What's that darling? What don't you mind?'

Despite Mike's efforts to engage in conversation, Lisa was still embroiled in a battle to save her unplanned innovation. *A Victoria Brick Cake.* Sadly, not a traditional *Victoria Sponge.*

Mike's collection of case studies made the impact of digital technology real. The stories grounded in life made them all-the-more special. The scale of impact and the speed at which things could happen were incredible. It seemed that new disruptions were happening at the blink of an eye, and on a scale even the most optimistic of forecasters could not predict.

'I know,' Lisa concluded, 'I'll cover it in custard and serve it as dessert. I'll just scrape off some of the black bits once it's cooled.' She sat down, a little happier than before and picked up the conversation with Mike.

'So that guy; the one we were talking about yesterday; tell me more about him. The one who first invented the term *Digital Innovation.* Where was he from again?'

Mike introduced Clayton Christensen, the father of disruption theory. A few minutes into giving more of Christensen's background, Lisa stopped him with a completely unrelated question. She'd lost interest for now.

'Is Charlie coming to dinner tomorrow night? Any sign of a girlfriend?' Lisa was curious to know.

'There's been no time for girlfriends since we set up our new technology company. Oh, and we've finally come up with a suitable name.'

'Go on, wow me!' Lisa begged, tongue-in-cheek.

'*3D*. It's stands for *Disruptive Digital Development*.' Mike felt quite proud of the name.

'And you had the cheek to make fun of my cake, when you've gone and named your high-tech company after a bra size?'

'Come to think of it, I never thought of that,' and they both laughed.

'So, has *Bra Size Limited* got any new ideas?'

'It just so happens that Charlie and I have been working on something new.'

'Let's me guess. Bras with Wi-Fi or GPS.'

Mike thought for a moment.

'That's not a bad idea. Wearable technology. Let me write that down.' He scribbled in the little black book he always kept with him. 'Lisa, my darling, you are a genius just like Clayton Christensen - only much more attractive.' Mike came close, put his arms around her and kissed her gently on the lips.

'I'm glad to hear it. Now can we go get a new oven? I need to be able to bake a cake or something resembling a cake, for dinner tomorrow night. Remember I bet Charlie a few weeks ago that I could do it. He said I couldn't.'

'Remind me, what was the prize, or should I say, forfeit?'

Lisa replied.

'If I win then he'd have to make dinner for four, in real-time with no practice. Just instructions. Ingredients and one hour.'

'And if you lose?'

'I have to lend him your Mercedes for a week,' she laughed, enjoying the wind-up.

'Let's go buy that new oven. The thought of another one of those *Victoria Brick Cakes* wrapped in rubber-like custard is a real turn off.'

As he passed, Lisa playfully clipped him across the head, to her own amusement. It was like being back in his school days when a teacher would clip him across the head for being cheeky or insolent. He'd forgotten about Leonard Tall for now.

Chapter 3

The owner and managing director of the TechWatch TV Studio, Derek Creswell, had spent much of his career in the media. The TV Studio was his pride and joy and the aptly named *TechWatch,* a weekly program about technological innovation, was the jewel in his crown.

Whilst successful, it was not yet prime time TV but was the most popular technology-focussed television programme in the United Kingdom. It regularly attracted viewing figures of 850,000; not quite reaching the elusive one-million mark that would elevate it into the TV Top 50, but it did at least give a healthy investment return through advertising, international licensing and sponsorship.

Fronting TechWatch was lead anchor Lenny Tall, a charismatic but arrogant forty-four year- old. He'd despised the first name *Leonard* given to him by his parents preferring *Lenny* in his professional capacity. Lenny had helped raise the audience to the current level since his arrival, but it was also conceivable that he was the main reason the one-million target had not yet been reached.

Lenny was born in Devon, and even from his early days, he'd been a troublesome kid. His parents sent him to public school in the hope that a good education and mixing with boys from well-rounded families, might turn him into a fine young man with the potential for a great career ahead of him in politics, as a captain of industry, or even in the military. A public boarding school had been found in desperation and his parents had hoped for the best, but knowingly, expected the worst of outcomes. As expected, Lenny did not take the bait and despite his parents' wishes and dreams, he turned out to be a bully with a surfeit of painfully annoying arrogance on top.

Despite his flaws, Lenny was a reasonably good student and was popular with the other boys, but he also possessed a competitive streak that often crossed the line between healthy competitiveness and manipulative domineering. He was good at running, but his best talent was in fluent, highly arrogant, bull-shit and being able to talk his way out of any situation. It was a talent he took to new levels when he took his first job in media at the age of twenty-one.

After ten years moving from job to job around the industry, he got lucky, winning a talent contest sponsored by a national radio station. Consequently, he was given his own one-hour daily show talking about trends, whether they were in fashion, music, sport or technology. Lenny's career was launched but after a few months he got bored and wanted to move on. He knew that he wanted more. He wanted television.

After sticking it out as he put it, he applied for a role at the TechWatch TV Studio. He always believed he was too good looking to be out of public eye, such was his self-belief and arrogance. He didn't want to be sitting behind a microphone. He wanted to be front and centre, where he could look straight into the eyes of an adoring national viewing audience.

In the final stages of interviews and studio tests, Lenny was pitted against a young, upcoming journalist called Lizzy Dawn. Lizzy was great in front of camera and conveyed a smart, eloquent confidence. During her screening tests, Lenny connived his way inside the studio to get a first-hand view of the competition. No-one behind the camera noticed him in an unlit corner or realised that he had tailgated an opened door. Lenny's competitive nature and hungry desire to be the subject of camera was everything.

When the time came for Lenny's screening tests, he took full advantage of his recently acquired insider knowledge, so easily managed to avoid replicating mistakes made by Ms. Dawn. Lizzy was sure she had spotted someone lurking at the back of the studio, but it wasn't until they were later formally introduced that she realised who she had seen. She wasn't too impressed by the way he'd stolen an advantage and was convinced he had cheated her out of the job. She felt that her industry awareness had been over shadowed by this ego-on-legs, but to Lenny it was just an arrogant and snidey hard luck, tough cheese inevitability over his appointment when they shook hands later, but Lizzy knew the score. He'd cheated and couldn't be trusted!

After Lenny landed the job of lead anchor, and seeing rich potential in Lizzy, Derek Cresswell invited her to become Lenny's assistant on camera. This she accepted, but with mixed feelings. Working with this sly, arrogant character would be a challenge but she quietly hoped that one day he would trip himself up, as his type regularly did. From now on she, would respect his position as TechWatch Lead Anchor, but not trust him as a person.

Chapter 4

After ringing the doorbell, Joanne could hear fast approaching footsteps hammering down on the hallway's wooden floor. Lisa opened the front door and after a few shouts of joy and lots of hugs, she invited Joanne in.

'Thank you for coming, and with just a day's notice,' she said delighted, whisking away her friend's jacket.

Charlie had arrived already and was tucking to a few snacks whilst savouring an oak-aged Chablis. He was chatting away to Mike as Joanne was quickly manoeuvred into the kitchen.

'Hey everyone, this is Joanne.' Lisa announced as she plonked her new guest on a bar stool next to the fixated snack muncher, Charlie.

Charlie had been forewarned about the blind date (or so he called it) and was pleasantly surprised to finally encounter Lisa's enthusiastically talked-up friend, Joanne Daley. Conversation was light; mostly about the weather, and then briefly about the luscious tasting wine that was being equally savoured by them all.

Lisa excused herself to fetch refills for the snack bowls, and Mike joined the other two in conversation. He was warned lightly not to ask Joanne too much about her job because she didn't like talking about it, so the conversation ebbed and flowed between he and Charlie while Joanne chatted with the returned Lisa.

First, the guys talked about football, and then rugby. For a short moment it was the latest movies and then politics. Eventually their talk turned into a more discrete exchange about their new app and other related news. Mike told Charlie that he read in the technology news, a couple of days ago, that Yeong Ji-Won, someone Mike had met the previous year, was on the verge of announcing his revolutionary Smart City System. Joanne's ear's pricked when she heard the words app and revolutionary mentioned. Turning away from Lisa she faced the two men and spoke with an unexpected confidence.

'So, what's new in technology? I hear you're developing a new and exciting app?'

Mike looked at Lisa who glanced back as if to say, it wasn't me, which was true. Lisa hadn't mentioned what they were working on to Joanne. Their guest had simply picked up on the conversation, noting the keywords in the exchange, as she had been professionally trained to do.

'It's not that big a deal. Ah, here comes dinner, I'm starving.' Mike side-stepped the question, as Lisa laid out food out in front of them.

Dinner was informal and served around the kitchen table. The wine flowed. Charlie and Joanne seemed to be getting along fine and laughing equally at each other's jokes. Everyone complemented Lisa on her cooking and Mike on his choice of wine before Charlie popped the all-

important question as he slurred slightly, enjoying the moment.
'Well my dear Lisa, how's that cake of yours? Did you manage to create another *Victoria house brick?*' This time Lisa looked at Mike, a stern not so happy expression etched on her face.
'Well my dear Charlie, I'm very pleased with my *Victoria Brick Cake* which you all just enjoyed for dessert, but now that you come to ask, I've prepared something a little extra.' She reached into a cupboard and pulled out a very large Tupperware container. Standing back from them, with arms and hands stretched across two corners, she peeled back the lid.
'Wow! That looks amazing,' exclaimed Joanne.
Mike was equally impressed, and Charlie was gobsmacked. In all the years he'd been coming to their house he'd never thought she'd been capable of producing such a show-stopping cake.
'Well, Mr. Charlie Duke, I think that's that. Over to you. No car lending this week! Or Ever! It's game over - except it's not.'
Lisa paused, pulling in her excitement at defeating Charlie in their fun little bet. She had turned the table on him.
'So Mr. Charlie Duke,' the wine now effecting her speech, 'you… now… have… to… make…. dinner… for… four! Us four! Right?'
Charlie smiled and rolled his eyes. Having conceded as subtly as possible, he picked up chatting with Joanne again. He wasn't going to give Lisa any more of the limelight. Besides, he was far

more interested in the other lady at the table. The oak-aged Chablis had been replaced by a mellow Merlot and everyone was now freer with their speech. Joanne tried her luck again.

'So, tell me about this great new app, I'd love to learn more.' She was surprisingly alert for someone who had put away nearly a whole bottle. Charlie answered, ill-advisedly eager to impress. He explained a lot of what they were doing, much to Mike's disliking but after five minutes, he too picked up the story.

'It's like this Joanne; there could be one hell of a bombshell hitting the market later this year, if the insurance industry doesn't wake up and smell the coffee.'

'Coffee!' shouted Lisa, reminded of the fresh pot she'd just made. She left Joanne talking with the men.

With the evening almost over, Charlie and Joanne exchanged numbers, thanking each other for their company. As they left, both expressed appreciation to Mike and Lisa for their hospitality, then shared a taxi across to the other side of the city. After daring conversations and laughter on the way, they eventually flicked a coin to decide whose bed they'd wake up in next morning.

In the days that followed, Joanne (now Jo to Charlie), eventually asked a favour of him. Her son, a full-time student, was looking for work in software and was specialising in information security. Charlie was happy to agree. He'd needed someone to help with the workload anyway, good or bad. He was just pleased to help Jo, and her son.

Chapter 5

As a supermajor, with developing green energy credentials, the vertically integrated oil and gas producer Sand Oil and Gas, dominated the UK fuel market with around one-quarter of a million employees spread over twenty European countries, with worldwide operations encompassing seventy more across the globe. The company owned several oil and gas producing fields in the North Sea, with experts forecasting their near depletion within fifteen years. Worldwide, the picture was not much better with oil expected to run out within twenty-five years and the global supply in around fifty. With Dubai having already shifting their major focus from oil exports to tourism, it was a clear sign that change was coming, and soon.

With increasing environmental demands, fluctuating oil and gas prices and margins being eroded by Russian and Chinese competition, plus the increasing supply from emerging markets such as those of South America, Sand Oil and Gas was aiming to diversify further into alternative energy sources. To this end, previous CEOs had considered acquiring utility companies, an automotive business, and even moving into financial services but every time they wanted to make a move, another market crisis would hinder their progress. First it was the Millennium Bug of the year two thousand, then the internet bubble, and global instability in the wake of 9/11, which were quickly followed by the launch of the smart phone and tablet. By the time the financial crisis broke in 2008, Sand Oil and Gas's diversification plans had been thwarted several times.

The 9/11 terrorist attacks brought a new focus to disaster recovery and contingency planning while global security became the number one focus for most countries. The threat of terrorism increased worldwide and with ISIS extending its reach and influence in the Middle East, it was no wonder Sand Oil and Gas had plenty to keep it busy. Adding to these concerns, combined tensions between the UK, Europe, Russia, Syria, Yemen, Iraq, Iran, North Korea, China and the United States, meant international cooperation was at an all-time low. With Donald Trump in The Whitehouse, eager to change the status quo, each day the world faced both the cumulative effect and implied impact of multiple crises.

Frank Delaney, the current Sand Oil and Gas CEO, was quietly thinking and pondering the cumulative impact on the global market. 'If the whole world put their domestic and international problems to one side, shook hands and started working together, Sand Oil and Gas would still have to face its major operational issues and an uncertain future.'

Whilst most of these problems were outside of his control, it was well known that maintaining oil and gas supplies dominated government agendas, and often became the target for new regimes after an overthrow. Frank continued to ask himself some key questions.

'How can we best reduce carbon emissions? How can we work with environmentalists while also keeping shareholders happy?'

The company's problems also extended to retaining staff in countries suffering unrest due to security threats and risks, as well as keeping leading politicians sympathetic on fuel duty, corporation tax and pollution. On top of all these concerns, Frank had to figure out how Sand Oil and Gas could remain valued by their customer base. Shaking his head ruefully, he reflected on the company's developing track record in converting to and implementing greener technology. The world at large seemed to ignore the fact that despite the heritage name, Sand Oil and Gas was a global leader in the use of, and investment in, green technology. Their solar, biofuels, tidal, hydrogen, electricity and water driven turbines still represented a small percentage of overall business but nevertheless it was leading the market.

Frank recalled his most recent meeting with the Chancellor and his speech to industry captains the previous Autumn.

'The UK government lacked the leadership to set clear, unambiguous policies for the adoption of new greener technology which would forge a pathway to the future. Sand Oil and Gas, traditionally on the wrong side of green, needed support from the government to move away from carbon-based fuels, and more aggressively pursue the adoption greener technology.'

The government's policy was one of obstinance and subsidy cutting, declaring that it was:

'The duty and responsibility of all companies to make their own way to the future and not seek handouts from government.'

Frank recalled his personal stance and Sand Oil's argument at the time.

'That government was ignoring the needs of the public, and that it had a duty and responsibility to incentivise the public. Examples such as ending the green energy subsidy scheme and closing the feed-in tariff for new solar panel fittings gave the wrong message. The public needed to be encouraged to switch from fossil fuels to more sustainable energy and greener transport technology.'

The situation was currently at stalemate, with neither industry nor government conceding. The public continued to buy carbon emitting vehicles because the cost of *green* cars was too high, and the country lacked the infrastructure to support them. He recalled similar arguments from the telecommunications industry about mobile phone and broadband coverage.

Frank Delany felt the burden heavy on his shoulders. He was at the helm of Sand Oil and Gas and was the person charged with finding solutions to the long list of complex company problems. He'd been appointed CEO shortly after the financial crisis of 2008, and he'd ably steered the company through the difficult period of recession that followed. While there had been some job losses during the period, they were due mainly to internal efficiencies and the closing of less profitable offices and operations across the world. Frank continued to restructure parts of the company, reduce overheads, and was continually searching for affordable and synergistic opportunities to diversify the company. He figured,

'Everyone would be happy then; shareholders, employees, suppliers, the public and the politicians. Even his wife would be happier!'

He was more than competent in his role as CEO, but he found it onerous. He wanted to solve all the company's' problems and leave a substantial legacy. He needed to do something radical soon, to begin the process of securing the future of the company and the livelihoods of the half million people under his leadership. The questions were always the same.

'What can I do, and how can I solve these problems?' He didn't have the answers.

Glancing over the company figures once more, he allowed himself a little smile and felt a sense of satisfaction. Growth was steady, costs were down and investment in the new self-service infrastructure was beginning to pay off. Whilst numbers were still low overall, more people were switching to greener cars, electric and hybrid, despite the government's incentive shortfall. There was no green revolution, but more an evolution, and it was arriving very slowly. Looking at the forecasts he concluded:

'Within the next fifteen years, the green market will reach the 50/50 tipping point with sales of oil, diesel, petrol and oil-based goods, which will then be overtaken by green technology, and the dependency on fossil fuels would continue to reduce year on year.'

Frank knew his company was under threat; not at this moment, but in the long term. There was 'no need to panic', he told himself, but he would have to sow seeds of change soon in order to bring about his revolution before it was too late. He must act now and convince the Board of his plans - he mulled over the strategy again and again. There was plenty of time to do something radical, but Frank knew from experience that proper, transformational change took time, perhaps several years, and that the benefits take much longer to accrue. Perhaps the full fifteen years?' he considered.

Frank's intention was to raise the subject at the next full board meeting and seek support for his latest strategic plan. But he wasn't convinced his plan was strong or cutting-edge enough to transform the company and secure its future. He was struggling to come up with something truly transformational; something no-one could resist, something that would increase sales and tie people in for long enough to allow the company to diversify into other markets. His plan included the acquisition of several green energy companies of the future but as he had *nothing radical* in the strategic plan, but needed to act soon, he started to consider bringing in a consultant or two to help the company crack that nut.

'There must be something out there that will allow Sand Oil and Gas to diversity without paying a premium, or expensive consultants to do so, but what? If only we could leverage the assets we have today?'

He thought, deeply pondering with his own mind.

As he read his strategy presentation one more time, Frank reflected. He was planning to ask for £100bn in investment over the next 5 years, with much of it going on technology, early stage start-up businesses, the acquisition of several small green energy firms, and for the research and development of new oil and gas fields, the latter becoming more and more challenging with the increasing burden of UK regulation, political uncertainty, ongoing corruption and environmental restrictions. The life of an oil and gas CEO was not an easy one - Frank never asked for easy, just a level playing field. He stared out of his large office window across the London skyline, giving a small sigh. He shrugged his shoulders, telling himself to stay positive.

'Something amazing might happen. Let's hope so,' he wished, 'let's hope so!'

Chapter 6

TechWatch, the TV rival to Channel 5's The Gadget Show, attracted a strong audience from the start, and with technology's seemingly unending, break-neck rate of change, viewers' appetite for the latest in tech news remained voracious. Although the format hadn't changed much in years, different tweaks had been made to help increase viewing figures.

Probably the most notable change was the development of a proactive fan base after the programme and TV studio launched their website, followed by a Facebook page with over 300,000 followers and a Twitter account soon to reach 500,000. Not exactly at Kardashian levels but social media had proved highly worthwhile in building an audience, and the TechWatch team regularly interacted with followers and viewers to keep them positively engaged between programmes. It was a great source of feedback and helped fuel ideas for future programme topics.

With the proliferation of smartphones and tablets, followers and viewers grew more adept at understanding the value and benefits of digital technology, and the team were often asked their opinions on wearable technology, drones, artificial intelligence, robotic toys and, of course, apps! It was Lenny and Lizzy's responsibility to stay informed about technology trends on social media and to interact with followers when not on air. Lizzy loved it but Lenny wasn't a fan. He tried rationalising away his part in it, saying 'it was Lizzy's bag, as his assistant.'

His unconvincing gust of "I am the front-man, not the back-office administrator", would be flatly met with the derision it deserved. But Lizzy was smart. Being the only presenter with an online presence meant she was more in touch with viewers, enjoyed the interaction and consequently developed a wider grasp of tech developments and trends. Lenny, on the other hand, just read the autocue and lazily relied on Lizzy to keep the show together.

Not long into Lenny's contract, Cresswell was gradually forming fresh opinions as he became aware of Lenny's antics. By contrast, he recognised the hard work and dedication shown by Lizzy. She was by far the professional in the ranks. Derek knew it, so did Lizzy but with Lenny seemingly still the popular front man, the station held back from making any drastic changes.

The TechWatch format was straightforward. Lenny would lead with the big news items for about ten minutes. Then the phone lines would be opened, and viewers' calls would be taken live on the show. This was when Lenny would generally pass the buck, expecting Lizzy to fill in, while he concentrated on looking charismatic and as important as possible on camera. Occasionally, a question would be directed at Lenny, but he always found a way to deflect. That is, until a viewer announcing himself as David Michaels, called in.

'Mr. Tall, I'm a little confused and I need some help.'

'You're talking with Lenny. Go ahead David.'

'Can you explain the meaning of NLP?'

Lenny hesitated, discreetly looked at Lizzy for usual sign she would take the question, but for once, Lizzy purposely avoided eye contact, leaving him to flounder. Lenny realised he had nowhere to hide, so turning back to the face the camera, he attempted to brazen his way through.

'David, I think you might have the wrong programme. We talk about technology here, not politics. If you want to talk about the National Liberal Party, try calling Radio 4 instead,' he blurted, feeling far from certain that there even was such an entity.

'Thanks for your call David, better luck next time,' he said, before quickly moving on. 'Lizzy, over to you.'

Lenny settled back, continuing straight-faced but blanking out the last minute or so. Lizzy was seen by Derek Cresswell to mutter *OMG*, just off camera. As camera one switched to Lizzy, she picked up where Lenny left off.

'Always a great sense of humour Lenny,' she said, trying to appear as relaxed as possible. 'Just in case you didn't get that, NLP stands for Natural Language Processing and is a specific area of

Artificial Intelligence or AI. Thanks for your question David, please call again.'

After each show ended, Lenny would disappear, while Lizzy would usually go to her desk and replay the programme looking to see how it went, trying to identify things that could be improved. Derek too would stay behind to critique the performance, but this evening, as soon as the mess had ended, Derek asked Lizzy into his office.

'I want to thank you for stepping in to cover for that prick. Even I could have explained NLP! I think it's time we looked at giving you a promotion. Leave it with me and I'll give it some thought. In the meantime, just keep up the great work.'

Walking back to her car, Lizzy thought about the evening's events. She beamed at the owner's feedback but wondered if anything would come of it. She'd worked in Lenny Tall's shadow for many years. Promising thoughts raced through her head.

'Maybe my time has come. Maybe it's time for Mr. Tall, to fall over?' she sniggered.

She had a great boss in Derek Cresswell but a real idiot for a lead anchor. Hopefully, things were about to change.

Chapter 7

Anna checked her email again. There was nothing from Marku. She was very worried. It was unlike him to not talk with her each day. She scrolled through her mails one more time, hoping she'd missed something.

Vasile, her boyfriend, didn't speak. He remembered the last big argument he had with Marku and felt it wiser to say nothing which was his way to keep the peace. Instead, he made coffee and brought a full mug to her as she sat on the sofa, her laptop balanced on her knees.

Vasile Lupei, otherwise known as *The Wolf,* was an internationally-known cybercriminal. He'd made quite a bit of money over the past years sending out phishing emails and blackmailing large companies into handing over cash with fake invoices and the use of ransomware. Occasionally, just the threat of a distributed denial of services (DDOS), when ghost computers bombard a website with millions of fake messages causing them to crash, would be enough to get him what he wanted. He would call off the DDOS when he could see the demanded sum had arrived in a laundering account in Switzerland. After reaching an offshore bank account, the money was then transferred to another bank account in Monte Carlo. Through all of his cybercrimes, he had managed to amass a small fortune, enough to buy a nice house in England and to live comfortably for a few years.

As a cover story, Vasile was an expert website and app developer. He maintained this so-called charade by having a few well-known clients that paid him well to improve their websites and apps, and specifically the security. He was good, but not brilliant. He'd taught Marku everything, but Anna's brother had soon showed signs of extraordinary talent. As a public awareness of cyber security increased over time, it was getting progressively hard for Vasile to make good money. He put pressure on Marku to help him go in deeper, but his protegee continually refused. That's when the arguments started. At his height, Vasile had been one of the most successful hackers in Europe.

'I am The Wolf. I track, I hack, and I pounce on my victims!' He would tell himself, enjoying the self-proclaimed air of notoriety.

Authorities across Europe knew him well, but they could never gather enough evidence or catch him in the act to make an arrest. Feeling compromised by Marku having left and then disappeared, he decided that soon he would step back from cybercrime and take stock. But first, he needed one last big scam to bring in enough money to last a life time. He could then spend all the time he wanted in England and Monte Carlo.

Anna clutched her mug of coffee.

'I will send him an email with the *Read Delivery* switched on. At least then I'll know he's alive, even if he can't answer for the moment,' she thought.

Again, Vasile said nothing. He knew that just because someone had opened an email, it didn't mean for certain that the reader would have been Marku. Afterall, his laptop could have been stolen or his email hacked. A couple more days passed and there was still no word from Marku. When Vasile was at work that morning, Anna had made up her mind. She was going to England to find her brother. She called Juliana, an old friend from her village, who was working there. There were shrieks and laughter as the two friends re-connected, but the mood quickly darkened when Anna explained the reason for her call. Juliana also knew Marku and about the close relationship he and his sister shared.

Juliana had moved from London to the South Coast and was enjoying life close to the beach in Weymouth, Dorset. Life was busy and the many tourists in the town created opportunities for work as well as play. It was arranged that Anna would take a flight to Heathrow, then get a train to Paddington Station. Then it would be a taxi to Waterloo to catch a direct train to Weymouth. She and Vasile had talked about moving to England to start a new life away from cybercrime. She quietly reflected on her dilemma.

'But he's always so tied up with his activities and his next project - he never makes time to talk about it like two adults.' She frowned. She was hatching a plan and would reveal it to him over lunch today.

Lunchtime came and went. Vasile did not object to Anna's plan. Instead he saw how much she was missing her brother and inside was feeling some of the guilt, knowing he was the cause for Marku leaving in the first place. Instead they hugged and kissed, Anna crying on his shoulder. That afternoon Anna called Juliana to finalise the arrangements and talk about life in Weymouth, and the possibly of getting a small job to cover her costs while she searched for Marku. Juliana mentioned that Weymouth was quiet now with very few tourists but there was a job going at a very nice café in the nearby town of Dorchester, only four miles from where she lived in Upwey.

After an emotional goodbye to Vasile, Anna took her flight to London and then caught a train to Weymouth, where Juliana met her on the platform. For a while, Anna put her Marku troubles to one side, as she excitedly discussed dressing up and going out for a celebration with Juliana.

At New Scotland Yard, Marku Sala was beginning his new life as Adam Barth, the freshest member of the cyber security team. After painlessly completing his induction training, his new boss Joanne Daley had called him to her office for a briefing. His first assignment would be simple. He'd been enrolled at one of the local universities to study Computer Science. He was to attend lectures and complete any course work just like any other student. After a few days he was to introduce himself to Charlie Duke, who ran a local development company called 3D with his partner Mike Day. The objective was simple; work with Duke on the app, add essential access controls and encryption, then with their full knowledge, set a trap for the intelligence service's primary target, a renowned and to this date, highly evasive cybercriminal.

Her code name was *Mother,* and she would refer to him as *Son.* This way any conversation between them would be regarded as perfectly normal and not raise any suspicions. At the end of the assignment, she would tell him it was time to come home, and he would then follow the pick-up procedure outlined ahead of time. It was too early to trust him with details on any target. Jo called Charlie, to put him in the picture.

Charlie couldn't remember if he'd come across Adam during the term so far but wasn't concerned because he didn't always get to know all the students by face or name, so shrugged it off. He had been very busy lately with 3D and the app, so it was no surprise he still hadn't spoken, one to one, with all the students that might be in his department.

Charlie was always happy to hear from Jo. Things were good between them, even if they hadn't spent much time yet talking about backstories. When they'd meet, there were always better and more fun things to do than quiz each other on unimportant stuff like details of what Jo did for a living, or cobwebbed family anecdotes. Nevertheless, he was happy to help her son by letting him join his development team of hand-picked students. He'd introduce Adam to Mike later, but for now, he'd just wait for the lad to make contact.

Chapter 8

It was a bright, cloudless day in London as Mike made his way along the embankment to Somerset House. The Spring tide was high on the Thames and the river bustled with commuter boats. Overhead, screaming seagulls added to the vibrant buzz of the city. While he walked, Mike studied faces in the stream of commuters, hurrying to their destinations. Everyone looked serious, focussed, some looked stressed even though the working day hadn't really begun yet. He wondered how they might look on the return journey; distraught, panic stricken, tearful, lost?

The new recently added cycling lane was busy, and despite the large number of people on two wheels, traffic on the main road was as choked as ever. The congestion charge, introduced in 2003, appeared not to be the deterrent it had been designed to be. There were just as many cars and trucks crawling by as ever; just different drivers and passengers.

One day, he envisioned, cities would be smart, and congestion would be a thing of the past.

Mike sauntered past the fountains at Somerset House that bubbled, glinting in the thin sunshine. It was too early in the morning for children to be playing amongst them, but a deeply engaged group of Oriental-looking tourists were taking multiple selfies and photographs of the surroundings. With the British pound falling against most currencies since the vote to come out of the European Union, London and much of the rest of the UK, was benefitting from an increase in tourism.

At the entrance to Somerset House, Mike followed the signage for the UK Insurance Industry Annual Conference, eventually finding the desk for speaker registration. After picking up his name badge, he drifted into the auditorium, taking a seat in the front row as requested. The room was already quite full; predominantly male as expected, brown or grey suited but he could see a healthy spattering of female delegates too. He estimated an average age of say, thirty-five to forty. Last year, he recalled, it was closer to fifty.

'Maybe things are changing at last?' he thought.
'The younger generation seems to be coming through now, and maybe, just maybe, the seeds of change have already been sown?'

He suddenly caught a glimpse of the TechWatch presenter, but this time it wasn't a flashback. Lenny Tall was real. Mike watched as he held a one-sided conversation with the on-stage media team. He noticed how Lenny had aged, and that he didn't seem to be as lofty as he remembered him from their school days, but he still had the knack of creating a personality clash with his choice of clothes. A beige suite, white shirt and blue/green tie didn't appear out of place at the conference but would probably turn a few heads in the City.

At 09:00 sharp, the TV presenter took to the stage, introduced himself, then proceeded to warm up the audience with stories of insurance blunders and jokes about car drivers, especially women drivers. Lenny was enjoying himself. He'd always enjoyed ribbing others, as those who remembered him from his school days would attest. The conference was then formally opened by the Chair of the UK Insurers Association, and after some basic housekeeping, he introduced key note speaker, John Calcott, CEO of Insurance Direct, the largest insurance company in the UK, if not Europe.

Surprisingly as the leader of a major organisation, Calcott was an average speaker. His presentations lacked the expected charisma, energy and passion of someone in his position, and he rarely captivated his audience. Today, he talked about the industry, the outlook in terms of economics and the potential threats from emerging markets such as China and South America. He touched upon investment in research and development, the need for new products and better services, and commented on the busy roads of the UK, car crime and increasing competition, but let slip that Insurance Direct was reviewing its policy considering increased business risk, and the necessity to cover liabilities adequately. The impact of Brexit was looming, but he reported that the actual impact thus far from mainland Europe on sales and operations, had been relatively low, if at all noticeable. The extensive presentation ended. There was no question and answer session.

'Disappointing,' Mike muttered to himself, knowing how hard it would be to get access to someone like Calcott in such a public setting. He had so many questions to put to him.

Lenny Tall rushed forward like a greyhound out of a trap. He vigorously shook John Calcott's hand and turned to address the audience.

'Now ladies and gentlemen, a short video about this year's UK Insurance Awards,' he announced, before returning to his chair.

The video wasn't that short: It was one of those run of the mill, shiny, music-pumped productions stuffed with the great work they were doing, in the hope of recruiting new members.

Peter Langley, an industry governance expert, delivered his presentation in the pre-lunch session. Langley was an impressive speaker. Articulately, he used a wide range of data to explain his points, and the impact of several possible outcomes from the impact of Brexit. Mike made notes. He talked about congestion, impact on the environment, trends and risks.

Langley concluded his presentation with an unbelievably quick summary. 'All the data suggests stable and steady growth, an increase in premiums, relatively low impact from new market entrants.

The current outlook is positive. The one big unknown is Brexit.'

An appreciative round of applause followed the speaker to his seat.

Lenny closed the morning session. No sooner done, he headed off, still in greyhound mode, towards the breakout room where an elaborate buffet had been laid out. A few minutes later, having loaded his plate, Mike saw his chance to re-introduce himself to the boy from his past. He had no idea if Tall would remember him or if he did, would even acknowledge their shared past. Approaching Tall, Mike assumed he wouldn't remember or recognise him. With his hand out stretched he spoke.

'Hello, Mr. Tall, I'm Mike Day. I'm speaking this afternoon about what I see as the future of digital technology. Maybe you would like to interview me for TechWatch, sometime?' he asked brightly.

Lenny gave no sign that he recognised either Mike, or his name.

They shook hands briefly before Lenny turned his eyes back to the buffet table. Mike held out his business card in anticipation of a reciprocal exchange - Tall didn't!

'Still the same old Lenny,' thought Mike, recognising the familiar sense of self-importance from the presenter's demeanour and the ingrained arrogance that went with it.

'Let me have one of your cards,' jumped in Mike.

'I can give you a call sometime to discuss new technology ideas and threats emerging from the market place?'

Lenny was only slightly more interested.

'Okay, Mr. Day, let's talk when you have a story. Here, take one.' Mike quickly pocketed the card and left Lenny to enjoy his lunch.

A little later, when scanning the card to his phone, he read, 'Lenny Tall, Executive Anchor, TechWatch TV Studio, London, W1 5AZ, and mused on the title Executive Anchor.'

Remembering the Lenny, he knew from his youth he couldn't imagine him in any sort of Executive position.

'Well, that's just about as vacuous and as self-important as I would have expected from this fellow,' he grinned.

The card had no mobile phone number or email address, just a main reception number. Tall couldn't be bothered to take calls directly, so used the company receptionist to screen everyone and everything. He often referred to her in company as his personal assistant, a ploy his ego particularly enjoyed.

Chapter 9

On the south coast of England in the town of Dorchester, Gloria Stenson was completing the paperwork for one of her regular clients.

'Yet another renewal,' she confirmed to herself.

Gloria prided herself on knowing each of her clients personally. In her *Broker of the Year* acceptance speech at the previous year's UK Insurance Awards, she recalled talking briefly about the importance of the customer experience. She was certain that the main reason her customers returned to her year on year was because she always put them at the heart of her business. She laughed, remembering the little joke in her short moment of fame.

'Well if you can't get car insurance from Broker of the Year, who can you get it from?' The normally humble Gloria brought the house down. She was a legend.

When her customers came to renew their car insurance, and despite the unavoidable higher premiums, the excess and yet more exemptions and restrictions, they always signed on the dotted line. Business wasn't about price or even the policy, they just trusted Gloria Stenson, UK Broker of the Year. She just did her job, treated people with the utmost courtesy and they would renew with rarely so much as a raised eyebrow. She was a friendly, personable lady with a forthright manner that was softened by a surfeit of professional etiquette.

Gloria valued the traditional ways of doing things, like making the time to do business over a cup of coffee and a polite chat, but even she eventually succumbed to the computer as *an office must have*. She had delayed buying one for as long as she dared but with seemingly everyone now going online, she finally took the plunge. A local computer company was commissioned to select a laptop and printer to suit her needs. After installing all the peripheral paraphernalia, a quick training course and a few mishaps, she was becoming quite proficient in using it for emails, calendar appointments, quotes and many other basic tasks. Next month she was moving all her accounting online and upgrading to a new car insurance quote system.

With the increasing spread of communication technology, Gloria had realised that she could no longer get the latest insurance news and prices by directly calling the wholesalers. Everything was now online.
'Except fresh hot coffee,' she thought with a smile. 'Fortunately, some things will never change.'

Gloria lifted her laptop lid, hit the power button and waited for the system to boot. She enjoyed hearing the business-like whir of the in-built fan as the system came to life. It was sign - she was getting ready for the day's business. Leaning back, she switched on the coffee machine behind her, having pre-selected a Nespresso capsule number 7, her regular choice for starting the day. She disliked instant granules, preferring the rich aroma of this version of fresh coffee, which she claimed made her shop more inviting to potential customers. The lure of fresh coffee was always a draw, or so she thought.

Turning back to her laptop, and a few clicks later she was browsing newly arrived emails. There were several enquiries; two from current customers, and three from potential new prospects. She quickly acknowledged each one personally. No automatic default response from her. To Gloria customers were too important to have a robot create the first impression. Glancing at her appointments calendar her face lit up with delight.

'So many nice customers today. And Farmer Swan!'

From the well-planned list appointments in her calendar a series of reminders had been automatically triggered. She also noticed that her brother-in-law, Andrew Dodd, was due to have his car insurance renewed on May the first.

'That's a good start,' she thought.

Her website, developed some months earlier, was regularly attracting people from far outside Dorchester, and there were new enquiries from as far afield as Poole and Crewkerne. After reading each email again, she clicked on another browser tab and selected one of her frequently used comparison sites, GoCompare! After a while, she switched over to MoneySuperMarket, and then MoneySavingExpert. Lastly, she clicked through to a news website for the insurance market. Now up to date, and with empty coffee cup in hand, she was ready to face the day and her first customer.

The shop door was pushed open, the bell ringing to announce Mr. Singh's arrival on time at 9:30 A.M. He was smartly dressed, befitting his status as a successful, second-generation businessman, with his turban adding a burst of colour against his grey suit.

'Good morning Mr. Singh, how are you today? How fine you look!'

'Ah! Ms Stenson, I'm very pleased to see you once more. I am here to renew my car insurance and to talk a little about how you are keeping.'

'I am very well,' she confirmed. 'Life treats me with many blessings.'

Gloria had come to know Mr. Singh over many years and looked forward to the sashay of courteous words they would exchange at each meeting.

'I am very happy to be your servant sir,' she offered in her finest courteous way.

'Business first, then we talk about how life is treating you,' he responded.

Over the next fifteen minutes or so, Mr. Singh renewed his car insurance and expanded his horizons on the local Dorchester gossip. Gloria had many customers like Mr. Singh. Renewing car insurance was as much about the relationship, the conversation, and the delights of chit-chat and pleasantries, as it was about the premium. When the time came to talk money, the sum would have been reduced to a mere formality.

Mr. Singh left after forty-five minutes, wiser for the gossip, more knowledgeable about Gloria and considerably poorer because of the car insurance premium, but he was happy, and legally insured once more to drive his car for another year.

At 10:28, Mrs Bell arrived with her two West Highland Terriers, Bonnie and Clyde. Mrs Bell was never late for anything. By the time she sat down, settled the dogs on the soft carpet, and turned to face Gloria, it was the exact time for her appointment.

'Well now Mrs Bell, you do look a picture today, and Bonnie and Clyde are so jolly in your company.'

Gloria knew exactly how to complement Mrs Bell and put her into her most precious of moods. Despite having become a tad grumpy in her later years, Mrs Bell loved to be complemented on her disposition; another renewal, another very happy customer. After nearly half an hour and some chit-chat, Mrs Bell was on her way out the door, grudgingly followed by Bonny and Clyde who had been woken from their naps.

For elevenses Gloria had another coffee, this time with a capsule number 5 and a small amoretti biscuit. She enjoyed her moment of relaxation, savouring the aroma of the coffee and biscuit. Next up was Farmer Swan, a harder nut to crack than Gloria's first two customers. Farmer Swan rarely gave anything away. Rationing his use of the English language, he was light on words. Gloria had already anticipated his antics, so had prepared quotes for all his vehicles the day before. She had carefully checked out all the premiums and created a combined package for three cars, two tractors, one combined harvester and a new Land Rover.

The cool outside air rushed in through the door as Farmer Swan entered the shop. He doffed his hat, sat down, then Gloria pushed forward his renewal quote. He scanned the quote up and down several times. He ponderously scratched his head on the left, then the right, contorted his face and then looked up with a wry smile.

'You've missed out my new Land Rover,' he said with a perverse satisfaction.

'Farmer Swan,' said the insurance expert, assured of herself, 'if you look on the reverse, you'll see details of your new vehicle. I understand it is your 65th birthday next week and that this Land Rover is a gift from your lovely wife Isabell?'

Farmer Swan nodded in agreement.

'It's already insured sir. Mrs Swan took care of it, last week. And may I be one of the many people in Dorchester area to wish you a happy birthday!'

Gloria stood and leant towards Farmer Swan. She embraced him and then kissed him on the cheek. The sudden physicality surprised the farmer. He took a half-step backwards, firmly shook Gloria's hand and headed for the door, turning only briefly to convey his satisfaction with a tiny smile, and a farewell doff of his green tweet cap. Gloria knew this was as good as it got from Farmer Swan and she felt delighted with her morning's work.

She understood the importance of providing good service and keeping control of her business in this way. It worked well, and she was proud of her success. Over the years, the local board of commerce had given her several awards in recognition of her brilliant customer service. Gloria Stenson was an award-winning business woman, a status she both valued and enjoyed.

Of her twelve hundred plus customers, most were over forty. For the time being, she was being kept perfectly busy servicing those already on her books, but she knew that if she were to keep her business running for another few years, it was increasingly important to engage with the younger generation. She earnestly believed that by giving each customer value through providing a genuinely personal experience, then price would rank lower down the list of priorities. But young people were highly sensitive to price, and consequently, Gloria hadn't achieved the same level of success with the latest generation of car drivers. The big online firms attracted more business with their slicker and quicker websites, but she was a customer experience natural – it was the magic dust that lay behind her years of success.

Today was a typical working day for Gloria; three appointments in the morning, with three to come this afternoon. Spring and autumn were always busy, but summer just depended on who was home and who was away, and winter was hit-and-miss depending on the weather.
When the shop was quiet, Gloria would reply to emails and set up appointments. She kept a contact list of customers, their renewal dates, and so on. As each customer's renewal date approached, she would send each a goodwill email reminder that their car insurance would be due soon. Even after emailing, she would make a courtesy phone call nearer the time and look forward to the repeat custom.

At the offices of Disruptive Digital Development *(3D)*, the company set up by Charlie and Mike, Charlie was busy explaining everything to Adam, the newest team member who was joining that morning. Charlie hadn't mentioned anything to Mike yet about bringing the lad on board at 3D, as a favour to Jo, because he was waiting for the right moment; not that he expected it to be a problem anyway. After taking Adam through the app design, its supporting website, and the administrative backend, he left him instructions to work on his own design ideas for security, specifically to protect against cybercrime and hacking.

Charlie had just finished writing a short advert for the university's notice board, which would also be distributed to selected universities across the country. It read,

Testers wanted for new digital app.

Above average rates paid for completed work.

Send email with phone contact details to charlie@ddd.co.uk

iOS, Android or Windows OS smart mobile phone essential

Use of or access to a car is also essential.

He mailed it to the university website administrator with instructions on what needed to be done. He had also added the list of additional universities whose websites he wanted it posted on, trusting the administrator to do their job. By the middle of the afternoon, his inbox had received dozens of enquires from interested students. Scrolling through them all, he added each to a mailing list he'd planned for future communications.

'Good job that man,' he said to himself.

'That result deserves a coffee and a luxury chocolate biscuit.'

Reaching down to his desk drawer, he retrieved a square box of biscuits.

'And for my next trick - coffee!'

Standing at the coffee machine he remembered to text Mike with the message, 'Good news old boy. Have had a great response on the student crowd testing front.'

Chapter 10

As Charlie enjoyed his mini reward, Mike was being called on stage by compere, Lenny Tall. The introduction was short and curt.

'Mike Day – 3D!'

As the day's final speaker at the Somerset House conference, Mike couldn't wait to get on with his presentation. Reaching the lectern, his phone vibrated in his jacket, but he forced himself to ignore it until later and stood to face the auditorium.

Mike suspected Lenny had twigged who he was but shifted his attention to the awaiting audience. He felt relieved that the short introduction hadn't initiated a stampede for the exits, although from his new vantage point, he couldn't detect much life in the auditorium anyway. He became aware of a slight people-odour in the room and it was a lot warmer on stage than in the stalls. Checking his first slide was displaying correctly, be began.

Ladies and Gentlemen, my name is Mike Day. Professionally, I am regarded as a digital disruptor and this afternoon, I'm going to speak about two interconnected topics; firstly, the digital technology revolution that's occurring across industries, and secondly, the potential opportunities and threats this brings to the insurance industry.

Mike picked up the murmur of a few voices, quizzically responding to his last line. He paused, before continuing,

> My hope is that the insurance industry will embrace the future that I will outline for you shortly, then act with urgency to capitalise on such opportunities. Action needs to be taken to mitigate certain threats to ensure the survival of the industry, in the UK, Europe and beyond. Failure to do both will, in my professional opinion, have severe consequences for the future of this long-established industry.

The auditorium was mostly silent but with a few shuffles here and there as a few people stood ready to leave. Clearing his throat, Mike continued.

> So, what's happening out there? What is this digital revolution? And why is it relevant to all of you?

> The Digital Revolution refers to technology's advance from analogue electronic and mechanical devices to the digital technology we have available to us today. This era started during the 1980s and is ongoing. The Digital Revolution also marks the beginning of the Information Era and is sometimes also called the Third Industrial Revolution.

He looked up, catching one or two people shuffling lower in their seats as though getting comfortable for a nap. He raised his voice, aiming to deter them.

The digital revolution touches all our lives. It's even more impressive when we examine the impact social media giants such as Facebook, Instagram and LinkedIn are having on our daily routines. These platforms play an important role in society as they allow people to connect with the millions around the world, share details of their lives and have fun. But as an insurance industry, if you're not taking advantage of social media, then social media will begin to take advantage of you. A social media strategy is essential in today's world for everything from communications, sales, marketing, customer service and public relations. A badly executed social media strategy can be a public relations disaster and cost thousands to rectify.

Mike gave a couple of case studies and then moved on to give an overview of the history and progress of the iPhone, and Google's rival Android system. How some 4.2 million apps had been downloaded over 180 billion times, translating as 25 apps for every person on the planet. He now wanted to draw his themes together.

> *The insurance industry is aware of the benefits of mobile apps and many insurance companies are already offering apps to their customers. In fact, the global mobile insurance market accounted for nearly £26 billion by the end of 2017. But apps are only part of the transformation taking place across the globe, as well as here in the UK.*

Mike stopped for a moment. He felt the presentation was progressing well. Stress was building in his body, so he took a moment to breathe deeply to help some of the tension melt away. Across the auditorium, he was aware that more people were leaving, or talking with the person next to them. London's rush hour was already underway, and he mused that the 4pm slot was probably too late in the day to make a proper impact, with people wanting to get away before the streets became gridlocked again. With his thoughts drifting to the leavers and the chatterers, Mike's concentration dropped for a moment. There was a shout from the auditorium.

'Get on with it,' followed by a ripple of laughter. After a further breath, he resumed.

'And what about the opportunities and threats of digital technology?'

Mike activated a slide showing the potential for app uses in the insurance industry. The glossy image showed apps designed specifically for brokers, sales, customers, and claims adjusters.

Others were for individually managing travel and car insurance, and policies.

> *Apps through the Apple App Store or Google Play are part of our everyday life now, and insurance is an industry that can benefit from expanding the scope in terms of enterprise apps to support both work processes and customer service. In fact, the industry is encouraged to more aggressively embrace this technology.*

He then talked about competitor threats, new business models and cited case studies from Amazon moving into supermarkets and Uber into fast food delivery. He warned them that the clock was ticking. It was only a matter of time before one of these super giant companies decided to enter the car insurance market. He cited Amazon again.

> *If Amazon can sell goods of all description, then why not car insurance? How would the UK insurance industry cope with a super-giant taking significant market share?*

Mike took a sip of water, before summing up.

> *Businesses across the globe must adapt to or, better still, drive this change. If they do not, circumstances will force them to react, which could be when it's too late. For companies that embrace the opportunities of digital technology such as apps, big data and better customer*

> experiences, the benefits can be wide-ranging indeed. But, for industries that bury their heads in the sand and fail to drive new business models, while ignoring the emerging competition - watch out! It's only a matter of time before irrelevance is standing at their door. The message is - change or be changed, be aware of the new and emerging risks, and act while there is still time!
>
> Thank you. I encourage you to embrace the digital age and do it quickly.

As the last words left Mike's lips, he scanned the auditorium for signs of life. There was a brief round of applause. He could see people heading for the exits and others packing up their stuff ready to follow. There was no time for questions as the schedule didn't allow.

He wasn't going to dwell on whether his presentation came across well or badly. He had delivered it with his usual passion and directness. By the time he had returned to the floor, the front two rows were empty. He sat down to reflect for a moment. Despite what he had told himself, he felt uneasy. He couldn't tell if they had listened or were just padding out the afternoon, but he dearly wished there had been time for questions. Without that opportunity, it was hard to tell if his key messages had landed, which left him feeling critical of the organisers and their lack in this regard.

Lenny Tall appeared on stage for the final time, thanking Mike for his speech and reminding people to take all their personal belongings with them. If they weren't coming tomorrow for the awards, then he would see them next year and wished everyone a safe and speedy journey to wherever they were going. After Lenny had formally closed the day, Mike watched the leavers. He could feel a wave of despondency rising. His despondency soon turned to anger at the general sense of apathy in the auditorium.

'Sadly, it's their loss. And what a big loss it will be,' he said, shaking his head.

He was just standing up to make his way to the nearest exit, when a voice came from behind him.

'Thanks for your presentation Mr. Day. Do you really think people believe in all that digital scaremongering and project fear? And all that stuff about Amazon selling car insurance?' It was John Calcott, the keynote speaker.

'I see people using mobile phones every day and hell, my kids have got more apps than I've had hot dinners, but do you really think the insurance industry is at risk if it doesn't change?' It was a direct question. 'Next you'll be saying eBay is selling holidays!'

Mike turned to face him.

'It's like this Mr. Calcott, there will always be competition from within the actual insurance market and while that continues, there's little incentive for radical change. But what if competition comes from a different industry? What if this new competition's proposition was better than yours, and that of every other Tom, Dick and Harry in the car insurance industry? What would you do then? How would you survive?'

'That's simple Mike, we'd compete right back. We haven't been selling compulsory car insurance following the Road Traffic Act 1930, without learning a thing or two over the past one hundred years. We know very well how our industry works, what our customers want and where we are positioned in Financial Services. And then there's the Competition and Markets Authority; they wouldn't allow it! I know people and a quick phone call to the CMA can be quite useful at times.'

'Are you quite sure about that?' Mike asked, whilst thinking, 'arrogant prick!'

'As sure as I'll ever be! Good to see you. Thanks again.'

As Calcott charged off towards the Executive Suite and his media interview, Mike called out.

'And by the way, holidays are already being sold on eBay!'

Chapter 11

Staring wearily at the Go-Compare price comparison site on his laptop, Andrew Dodd was checking out car insurance options. He entered his personal information, the details of his car, and hit submit. Within a few moments he was presented with a long list of quotes from a range of companies. The cheapest comprehensive cover stipulated an excess of £750 and premium of £675 to cover the next 12 months. In disbelief, he scrolled down hoping to find something more reasonable, but the excess and the premiums grew higher, the further the page rolled.

'I paid £525 last year, and the excess was only £250,' he reminded himself. 'And even that was a bit steep.' He scratched his head, Stan Laurel style, and contemplated his next move.

Even including his protected no claims discount, the cost of car insurance had risen yet again. He couldn't hide his distain and frustration with an industry that just increased prices year on year. He closed his laptop, stood up and walked into the garden. His wife Kate was raking leaves and generally tidying up, now the worst of winter seemed to be behind them.

'Darling,' he said, trying to appear nonchalant. 'It looks like we might have to cut back a bit on a few restaurants and trips this year because the car insurance has gone up by £225, and the excess, even more!'

Kate threw him a quick glance.

'Maybe, we should take up cycling and forget the car altogether' she replied with an air of flippancy.

'Maybe,' trailed her husband, oblivious to her tone.

'Why not give Gloria a call to see if she can help? She's very good you know, voted Best UK Independent Broker of the Year, or something like that. I'm very proud of her and I hear she's up for it again this year. Why don't you give her a call or drive over to Dorchester and pay her a visit? Better still I'll come too. I might do a bit of shopping. I love that historic little town. Such a pleasure. Let's go at the end of the month before the insurance expires and see what's what?', said Kate, eventually coming up for air.

'Okay, we will go in a few weeks, then.'

Andrew hoped his wife would soon forget about their conversation because he didn't want to spend any time discussing car insurance with Gloria, her insufferable sister. It took him five years to break away from buying insurance from Gloria last time round and he still couldn't remember how he did it. All he recalled was Kate in one ear, Gloria in the other, and himself stuck in the middle, when all he was looking for was a simple car insurance quote for a sensible amount of money. It wasn't too much to ask,' he remembered.

'Let's hope I find something decent online before then,' he snorted. 'I'll look again before the end of the month. After all, the renewal date isn't until first of May.'

He could at least hold Gloria off until the last day of April, or so he hoped.

At the café in Dorchester, Anna Sala had settled into her new job. She liked the town. 'It would be a great place to settle down and have a family.' She remembered when speaking with Vasile a few days ago.

Dorchester wasn't that far from London. The cost of living was acceptable and in the short term staying with Juliana, was keeping her outgoings low. She had continued to search for her brother, Marku, and after rent, the return rail fares to London were her biggest expense. She figured that London was the best starting point from where to pick up Marku's trail, but to no avail. He had completely disappeared without a trace. Worse still he hadn't contacted her in weeks. Anna tried not to dwell on the possible fate of her brother, reminding herself that he had always been resourceful and naturally self-reliant. She also missed Vasile, so gave him a call to cheer herself up.

Vasile was in a good mood and before long Anna had forgotten about her worries. After the call she had gone back to work serving hot drinks and cakes in the café. She was so pleased. Vasile was coming to the UK at last and had hinted that it might be the right time for him to give up his profession and go straight.

   Joanne and Charlie saw each other quite frequently but Jo remained evasive about here line of work. Instead conversations drifted between the 3D app, her son Adam, and a possible holiday with them all together in the Summer. Privately, Jo regularly called Adam for updates on the app, the timings of the launch and to discuss his progress in adding a built-in, but hard to detect, security trap designed to capture their target. Everything was progressing as planned, but she desperately hoped Charlie would never discover the truth about Adam and the real nature of their relationship. As uncomfortable as it made her feel, an oath that bound her to the Official Secrets Act, meant that she had no choice but to keep this secret from him. In her mind, she tried to convince herself that she was not lying to Charlie. She was merely complying with the terms of her employment.

Chapter 12

Reading the news on his tablet, Mike couldn't help feeling annoyed as he remembered attitudes shown by delegates at the insurance conference. The general sense of apathy had confirmed for Mike the short-sightedness and complacency within the industry. He questioned whether his presentation had lacked impact, or if his key messages had been badly worded. Perhaps his method and delivery style had been too contentious, so easily dismissed by delegates as being speculative and pie-in-the-sky? In the end, he drew the same conclusion as last year.

'They don't believe digital disruption could happen to them. They're too big, they've all got websites and apps, so reckon they've got all the tech stuff covered. And while there's a never-ending supply of new customers, and renewals continuing year after year, what's the fuss? The car insurance industry has been around for almost one hundred years. What's the fuss indeed?'

Mike knew that the industry continued to grow in line with expectations, and was as strong as ever, but he pondered a significant truth for a moment.

'They have not yet been disrupted! There's been no real industry disturbance and they've not had to develop strategies or plans to counter such a threat.' He smiled.

'Let's see how things look for them in six-month's time, when things get a bit more interesting.' He mused on the business card exchange with Lenny Tall.

'Maybe, just maybe, that arsehole will come in useful very soon?'

Mike continued reading the news. Like most people these days, he rarely picked up a newspaper, except on the odd flight when devices were switched to flight-mode. Although the roll out of in-cabin Wi-Fi systems were well underway, the facility was still mostly the reserve of the American airlines and restricted to email only, because there remained a reluctance in some quarters because of perceived flight safety concerns, as well as possible electro-magnetic interference from mobile phone use. Reaching *Sky News*, he scanned the headlines. He started with business news and picked his way through the various stories.

'The banks are getting hammered again; another LIBOR scandal,' he noted.

'These guys never learn.'

Mike managed to find a brief mention of the recent insurance industry conference. The article provided a highlights summary and listed all who were recognised in the industry's annual awards. Mike read down the list of recipients and noticed that a woman from Dorchester had once more won the Independent Car Insurance Broker of the Year Award.

'I wonder how good you need to be to win that one?' he questioned out loud.

'I hope she's really switched on because things are about to change and change quickly.'

This, he was certain of, as the Sand Oil and Gas CEO came to mind.

'And very soon. Frank Delaney will learn exactly how.'

Mike carried on, dipping in and out of articles that interested him. In the technology section he noted that a revolutionary Smart City System was to be rolled out in Seoul, South Korea. He looked for the name behind the initiative. It was Yeong Ji-Won, the guy he and Charlie had discussed at dinner a few weeks ago. A special launch event was being held at a conference centre in Seoul next month.

'Hmmm, that sounds interesting. I'll give Charlie a call and perhaps a little trip might be in order?'

He saw a likely link between their app in development, and Smart City Systems, only he didn't have any details yet about what Yeong Ji-Won was up to. Mike was always on the lookout for breakthrough technology, especially when it involved the use of cars, which of course, played such a huge role in so many peoples' lives. He was sure Ji-Won's Smart City System would be linked to cars somehow, suggesting a very interesting and potentially feasible synergy between their respective companies. Finally, he clicked through to the cyber security section to read about recent data breaches. He learnt about a recent DDOS attack on a popular shopping website, as well as the latest known tactics being employed by Chinese cyber criminals. And surprisingly, Romania had emerged as a hot bed for launching cyber-attacks.

'Charlie and I need to stay aware of these potential threats. If we don't add protection to our app in the right way, it too could be disrupted in all the wrong ways - that would be a disaster!'

He picked up his phone, tapped a message out and sent it to Charlie. 'Must catch up on the app security design. Need full protection. Check out threats from Romania.'

Enjoying the mild irony of the situation, he repeated to himself.

'Even The Disruptor can be disrupted!'

Chapter 13

Frank Delaney was deeply involved in orchestrating changes across the various divisions of his immense company. His personal assistant arrived with the morning post. A large brown envelope was stamped *security checked* and had *Private and Confidential* written by hand across it. Frank sliced open the flap end and carefully drew out the contents. Carefully bound, front and back with 3D clearly visible on the front cover, he started to skim-read. Turning the pages one after another, his excitement and disbelief grew the more he read.

'Claire, can you come in for a moment?'

His personal assist retraced her steps until she was standing opposite her boss.

'Claire, can you call this guy, Mike Day, and ask for a private meeting,' he asked, hurriedly.

'Arrange something away from the office; maybe that room we use from time to time at the Canary Wharf Hilton. Don't book it in my full name, just Mr. Frank. I don't want people putting two and two together and coming up with ten. Oh, and arrange some light refreshments as well, please.'

Claire nodded, left Frank's huge office and called Mr. Day. Slightly disappointed it wasn't Frank Delaney himself, Mike was nevertheless pleased to receive the call.

'This is Claire Stone of Sand Oil and Gas. Mr. Delaney would like to meet with you to discuss your paper. Would tonight, at the Hilton, Canary Wharf, at 7pm be suitable?'

'That would be perfect,' replied Mike, trying to curb his rising feelings of excitement.

'On your arrival, make yourself known to reception and the concierge will guide you to Room 2. The meeting is booked in the name of Mr. Frank - not Mr. Frank Delaney - just Mr. Frank please, and make no mention of Sand Oil and Gas, if you don't mind.'

'No problem. The Hilton, CW at 7pm and ask for Mr. Frank,' Mike confirmed.

'Thankyou Mr. Day,' responded Claire. She hung up.

Slightly fazed by the prospect of meeting one of the UK's leading captains of industry, Mike checked his watch and began to work out his travel plans. Later, as arranged, Mike arrived in Canary Wharf, squinting skywards at One Canada Square's pyramid roof as he left the tube station. He walked briskly across the South Quay footbridge, turning his coat collar up against the chill gusts, a common feature in this skyscraper landscape. Once at the Hilton Hotel, he was guided to Meeting Room 2, where he knocked the door and waited.

'Mr. Day?' asked Delaney, opening the door and offering a handshake.

'Yes indeed,' Mike replied. 'Mr. Frank, I presume?'

After both men had confirmed their identities, they moved into the room making small talk. There was a fabulous view across to the main business district of Canary Wharf, with bustling commuters and professional business people wining and dining in the shadows cast by setting sun.

'Help yourself Mr. Day. There are some canapés, soft drinks and I happen to know there's some harder stuff in the corner fridge.'

Both men helped themselves and after pleasantries, Delaney got to the point.

'Mike let's go beyond formalities now. I was intrigued by your proposal and it's fair to say that I more than liked it. Truth be told, I'm blown away by such a radical concept, which is why I wanted to meet you so soon.'

'I was hoping it would grab your attention,' said Mike, feeling thrilled by Frank's initial response.

'Some of the figures aren't quite right but overall they're not far off, and the way you've clearly laid things out is great. As a strategy it's very compelling,' Frank continued. 'And the insurance figures? Where did you get those from?'

Mike smiled, 'There's an extremely helpful chap called Peter Langley. He's an insurance expert. Worked in the industry for years. He had a wealth of information just dying to be exploited. We sat next to each other at the recent UK Insurance Conference. After a few calls and exchanges of emails, he came good! Gave us everything we needed.' Frank was impressed with the diligence.

'Thank you. We tried to be as accurate as possible.'

'We?' Frank inquired.

'Yes, I have a business partner, Charlie Duke. We set up our company, 3D together. I'm the brains, and Charlie, is the brawn.' They both laughed.

'Well Mike, I think we're going to be seeing a lot more of each other over the coming weeks and months. Here's what I have in mind.'

Frank explained that he would like to circulate the Executive Summary tomorrow to the board of Sand Oil and Gas, ahead of the full board meeting later that week. He'd like Mike to come along and present the detail of his proposal. The CEO would be seeking the support of the Board to go ahead and implement the proposal in full, hopefully taking the decision to go forward that very afternoon.

'It's going to be that simple Mike. You present then take questions, you recess, then we consider and decide. If all goes well, you should have a decision within the hour.

'That's agreeable Frank. All I would ask is that the contents within the Executive Summary remain confidential.

'I understand Mike. You have my word that it will only be shared with board members and that the detail will remain confidential until you deliver your presentation.'

The men continued discussing the proposal's finer points, with Mike taking note of any areas for improvement. At 9:45pm, Mike left the hotel. Returning across the footbridge again towards Canary Wharf, a big smile spread across his face. There was a clear sky with only a few stars visible above the bright street lights and skyscrapers, and ahead he could still see rows and rows of people in bars and restaurants. He wanted to join them for a cold glass of Chardonnay but thought better of it. Instead, he headed for the underground station. He would be home in forty-five minutes. There was a busy day ahead tomorrow. He needed to stay focussed. It was not yet time to celebrate - he and Charlie would do that at a little later.

'Perhaps in Seoul,' he thought, 'out of harm's way.'

Chapter 14

Now at the technology news section, Mike was coming to the end of his usual morning read.

According to recent higher education statistics, there had been a marked increase in the number of universities now offering degrees that focused on digital technology.

Closing his laptop, with his early morning routine now over, Mike used his mobile phone to contact Charlie from his recent calls list.

Charlie was one of relatively few university lecturers with applied experiences in digital technology. Earlier that year, he and Mike had formed their development company called DDD or 3D – Disruptive Digital Development. Together they had worked on a collection of ideas but primarily on ways to disrupt the insurance industry.

'Well Charlie, I think it's time to do our favourite thing. Let's shake things up a bit and get disrupting!' Mike said, feeling like a bit of a rebel.

'So, what's happened?' quizzed Charlie. 'I didn't hear from you last night so figured things didn't go so well with Sand Oil. Also figured you'd be drowning your sorrows over a bottle of wine or two.'

'You couldn't be more wrong my friend. Delaney liked our little proposal. In fact, he liked it so much he's asked me to present it to the full board later this week. I'm now shitting myself, ha!'

'Bloody hell Mike. Why didn't you call me?'
'Simples. It was late. If I'd called you, you'd have been awake all night like me. I'm now wrecked and just about holding it together after a quick espresso. I need to get some sleep. Let's meet tomorrow. See you around eight tomorrow morning, usual place?'
Mike ended the call, a tired but happy man.

The following morning, Mike and Charlie met at Tony's Coffee Shop, about a ten-minute walk from the university. It was a cold morning. On the grass-lined paths, the crocuses heads had dropped, and a frenzy of daffodil replacements were already in bloom. Inside the café, Charlie was already seated close to the window, the bright sunlight streaming through. Mike pushed open the door and, as he approached, Charlie stood up to shake hands.

'Well old boy, it looks like you're finally going to get your day of reckoning,' declared the lecturer, as both men shifted slightly to get comfortable.

'Ain't I just! Those arrogant insurance buggers just don't see it coming.'

'To be fair, this disruption is not something most industries will ever see coming.'

'You are so right, but I just wonder if some of the more advanced banks, supermarkets, car or software companies might have already contemplated the possibility of other, wider industry threats from the likes of eBay, Amazon, Facebook and Apple. These big twenty-first century companies have incredible market penetration and massive followings, as well as huge customer bases. Imagine what would happen if Facebook bought a very large bank, or if Amazon decided to buy Walmart? The mind boggles. People need to wake up and realise that across all industries, competitor threats are no longer confined to just the traditional market players.'

Charlie raised his eyebrows, and Mike took a deep breath.

'And we still remember Blockbuster. If that wasn't a lesson in the use of technology, I don't know what was?'

They ordered coffee and a couple of pastries.

'Let's review the plan,' suggested Mike, before Charlie had opened his laptop.

'Yeah, yeah! And I have an update on the cyber security threats we talked about too.'

Charlie turned his screen around to face them both while they went through the plan, line by line. It had been drawn up in deep detail, with all the critical milestones and dates highlighted in capitals.

'Looks good Charlie, but what about the cyber stuff?' Mike remembered to ask.

'Well, it's like this Mike. To catch a thief, or in this case one or more cybercriminals, you must lay traps but not make it too obvious, otherwise it won't satisfy their egos. But at the same time, you don't want to make it too difficult because they might start trying other stuff to bring them the success they crave.' Charlie hesitated for a moment, gathering his thoughts before using intricate detail to explain the in-built trap.

'Charlie, I think that's brilliant! Where did you get the idea - or shouldn't I ask?'

'Well, students are a fuckin' useless bunch most of the time but occasionally, one bright spark comes along. He came to me with some mad ideas and I had him design it, create the code framework, then the developers did the rest. They simply dropped the new code into the app. It's bloody genius,' added Charlie.

'What time are you seeing the oil boys?'

'Two o'clock at their head office on the Embankment. It should be fun, and let's hope they buy it, otherwise Plan C it will be!' They both laughed. "Plan C" was short for "Plan Charlie," a little idea Charlie had come up with if "Plan M (Mike)" failed.

After discussing recent events in the news, and Mike's little chat with Lenny Tall, they shook hands and went their separate ways. Mike arrived at the Sand Oil and Gas head office at a quarter to two and asked for Frank Delaney. After a couple of minutes, he was met by Claire, Frank's PA, who escorted him to the lift and the seventh floor. As the lift moved upwards, Mike read the control panel, 'Floor Ten, Restaurant and Roof Terrace, Floor Nine, Executive Gym, Eight, Executive Suite, and Seven, Board Room! The elevator bell pinged, and the doors slid open.

'They're not quite ready for you Mr. Day. Can I get you a coffee or something else to drink?' Claire Stone enquired with her customary professionalism.

Just before 2pm, the board room was opened by Delaney.

'Welcome Mr. Day or shall I call you Mike?' asked Frank, thrusting out his hand. They shook and Frank guided Mike into the room, gesturing him to a chair at the end of the table.

The room was long but not dark like the many board rooms Mike had seen. before. It was sleek and modern with very large OLED screens lining both end walls. As he made his way to the chair, he noticed several large paintings on the wall, each displaying a scene from Sand Oil and Gas locations around the world. Once settled, and with laptop connected to the projector, he turned to look at the massive screen behind him, reassuring himself that the technology was working. He then sat and waited for the formal introductions.

'Mr. Chairman, ladies and gentlemen of the Board, it is my pleasure to introduce you to Mike Day. Mike has built a reputation for himself as an ideas man and a disruptor. In fact, if you hear of anyone being referred to in the tech press or in business as *The Disruptor,* they're more than likely talking about Mike. Today, he's going to talk us through the detail of his idea for significantly growing our revenues over the next five years, while diversifying the company into a totally new market. All yours Mike!' With that, he sat down, crossed legs and relaxed into his chair, exhaling gently like a yoga expert.

Mike had presented to many boards over the years but this time it was different, as it involved probably his most radically disruptive idea yet. He began by explaining what was meant by *Disruption* and why it was relevant to all industries. He shifted his focus to Oil and Gas, explaining some of the challenges that lay ahead, such as global warming, the strains on the environment, pollution, the cost of doing business, political manipulation and Brexit instability. From there, he moved onto the disruption itself and carefully explained the key idea, each stage and finally the anticipated results. After nearly two hours, Mike summed up, leaving the Board with one final point.

'Mr. Chairman, ladies and gentlemen, to close, I offer you a final thought from a favourite pioneer of mine who's been an inspiration over the years.

'James Allen once said, 'For true success, ask yourself these four questions. Why? Why not? Why not us? Why not now?'

Mike sat back down, readying himself for a barrage of questions. The clock ticked over to 4pm, and the room was silent for a few, seemingly endless moments. The Chairman started to clap. A lady immediately to his right followed suit and was soon joined by everyone else. The sound of approval went on for an age, or so it seemed.

As the applause faded, the Chairman asked for questions, which then came thick and fast. Mike bounced back with an answer for each, enjoying his moment in the spotlight. Then came a question about the levels of cyber security within the app, causing Mike to take a moment to gather his thoughts before responding. He had already dispensed with the formalities of correct address.

'It's like this. We all know cyber-criminals love nothing more than to break into company systems to either cause major disruption, try to steal as much as they can, or both. In particular, the credentials of anyone in IT within an organisation, who might have confidential user privileges, are particularly attractive. Steal such credentials and there is no need for any highly sophisticated deciphering techniques and tools. It's just like opening a window so they can get into a room from the outside, but to go any further, and perhaps become a real threat, they need to open a door from within that room to take them further into the building.

'But if they should happen to break through protocols to access this app via a window (shall we say), they will find no ordinary room. Once inside, they won't be able to progress any further, neither will they be able to crawl back out of the window either. We've created an entertaining little cyber game and we're certain any cyber-criminal worth their salt will unknowingly play along with it, just long enough for us to spring the trap.' Mike grinned, looking back at the person who asked the question.

'Madam', he added, 'our technology is highly secure, intensely monitored and powerfully alarmed, with a few added surprises of our own.'

After another hour or so, the questions and discussion came to a natural conclusion and Frank

Delaney invited Mike to step out of the room while the Board took his proposal to a vote.

After a shorter time than expected, Mike received a call from Delaney.

'Great presentation Mike! The Board has voted in favour of your proposal and we look forward to receiving progress updates on the time-scale you have outlined. Good luck and happy disrupting!' The line went quiet.

Mike paused to take it all in, then gave Charlie a call. His colleague answered almost immediately.

'So, what happened? Do I get to show off and invoke Plan C or is it humble pie for me?' Charlie waited.

'It's very humble pie my friend, with extra you were right Mike toppings. They gave us the go ahead and we can start straight away. They want updates as we discussed. We need to get a final Go Decision on the 30th April. It could not have gone better. And by the way,' he paused, 'that brilliant cyber trap game addition from your star student, worked a treat. Get that kid on the team full-time. There will be more for him to do as iOS and Android updates are released.'

'Already done pal. I figured it would be better to have him on the inside with a bit of cash in his pocket, than on the outside, potentially playing with our app.' Charlie was almost patting himself on the back for such a great decision.

'OK, so the 3D office it is tomorrow then, at 8 A.M. We have a plan to deliver and an industry to disrupt.' Mike reaffirmed before hanging up.

Claire had been standing by. She cordially invited Mike to take the elevator to the ground floor. This time she did not accompany him, but in parting, smiled as though Mike had just joined the club. With the elevator doors closed it began to descend. For entertainment, Mike rewound the names of each floor in turn as the elevator dropped lower.

Back on the street he took off his tie and walked along the Embankment, a breeze cooling his skin. He swerved here and there to avoid tourists taking photographs, and skateboarders enjoying their graceful, weaving freedom. It had been warm in the boardroom, but he'd kept his cool. Walking slowly, stepping forward without any real purpose, he reflected on how he had delivered this most important presentation; how he had answered the hail of questions, and now had the support of the Sand Oil and Gas Board.

'The Disruption Begins,' he thought. 'Not quite like Batman Begins - but near enough.'

Chapter 15

Since the dotcom boom and rise of smart mobile technology, the mainstream media increasingly dipped in and out of technology news, to answer and stimulate the public's interest in modernity, but also as a way of generating advertising revenue from the latest must-have gadget. The TechWatch team were stumped by the TV show's perceived inability to ever reach the magical one-million viewers, knowing passing this landmark would increase their attractiveness to advertising agencies with blue chip tech clients. With ears to the ground, the programme researchers attended international technology fairs, scanned the internet several times daily and read the corresponding competitor news in the hope of finding something truly outstanding. Face of the show, Lenny, answered his mobile phone.

'Hello, Mr. Tall, it's Mike Day. I've got a great story for you. Do you have 30 seconds for a quick briefing?'

Lenny hesitated.

'OK, I'll give you... 28 seconds!'

Mike laid his pitch out as succinctly as he could.

'And then Mr Tall, on the morning of the launch, the first of May, we'll give TechWatch an exclusive providing you air it as your main programme headline that day. In principle, do we have a deal?'

The phone line went quiet for a moment while the information fizzed and tripped wires in the presenter's head. He didn't understand the whole concept fully, but he loved the idea of a shockingly new idea, and best of all, it came with an exclusive that was all his!

'I'll have to run it past my producer, but in principle, I think he'll go for it.'

Lenny confirmed, despite having no intention of informing his producer at this time. Whether through slackness, inertia or, what liked to call his, fiendish brilliance, Lenny decided to keep this information to himself, then simply drop it into conversation when there were only a few days to go. Nonetheless, he knew the man in charge would find it almost impossible to say no after what Lenny had just heard. This anchor man would at last have his one million viewers - and then some.

'Okay!' said Mike.

'Text me later today when you are all agreed. We'll send over some papers for signing and keep this very simple; If you air in exactly the manner we have discussed, you will then have your headline grabbing exclusive. But if you don't, we will be forced to apply the terms of the agreement and sue for breach. Play ball and all will be well. Mess us about and we'll be seeking damages.'

Lenny was used to agreeing simple commercial terms. It was standard practice in the industry if you wanted that big news story, and he knew that playing ball was essential if he was to reach that, just out of sight, viewing figures target. He would tell Lizzy about it later, much later. Maybe never!

As expected, Mike received the acceptance text later that afternoon, so duly sent the paper work. Less than an hour later, Mike received email confirmation that Lenny had signed on behalf of TechWatch TV studio. Two signed originals arrived by courier the following morning, which Mike counter signed, returning one copy in an A4 manila to Lenny Tall by the same method. Despite the importance of the deal he had just struck, Lenny rarely bothered himself with opening mail, so as usual, left that administrative task to reception.
Elsewhere, and with better care and attention, Mike called Charlie,
'It's done. TechWatch is on the hook to provide exclusive coverage every thirty minutes from six 'til noon on the first of May, just ahead of the official launch.'
'That's great Mike! And Tall went for all of it, even the penalties if he, or they screw up?'
'Yes, but I can't help thinking he's acting on his own, but that's no concern of min. He's got the executive powers to act on behalf of the TV Studio, especially were there's a scoop and an exclusivity period, but let's hope that neither he nor his colleagues mess things up, or it could really dent the initial impact of the launch.'

Chapter 16

In the couple of weeks following the UK Insurers' Conference, the media reported news of new disruptive business ideas.

MyBankAccount™ launched a cloud-based virtual bank account to allow customers to create their own type of digital-only bank account. The account came with a variety of interesting features for a range of fees. The media raved about the features but were less flattering about the fees. Nonetheless, in the first week alone, more than 25,000 accounts were opened.

Another venture, ComplaintsBase™ launched a new type of portal that provided a simple means for customers worldwide to log a complaint about something that had happened to them. The portal was available in twenty-five different languages and was an instant success, much helped by timely flight cancellations from one of Europe's largest airlines. ComplaintsBase™ would then submit a class action style complaint on behalf of all complainants. One case into the airline, backed by 25,000 angry customers, saved the airline £,000s in administration time as well as potential lawsuits. The airline made an offer to ComplaintsBase™ who in turn paid their clients.

As he reached the end of his morning news trawl, the last news item really caught Mike's attention. It read;

Get lower car insurance by using our app.

It was a national supermarket promising to reduce car insurance premiums for better safer drivers. The app had to be used when driving, when it would use inbuilt GPS tracking to record driving behaviour then calculate minimum, maximum and average speeds. It would then award points for the appropriate speed for the surroundings but also deduct points for inappropriate speed. Points could be accumulated and used for in-store purchases.

'That's interesting,' he thought.

'Shame they spent all that money developing something that might soon be redundant. At least in the short term, someone will benefit.'

Then he thought again.

'Actually, there's no reason why this app can't run alongside our own for a while – we don't offer points for in-store purchases - but it's an idea. I'll talk with Frank Delaney about it.'

Mike opened his browser and chose one of his favourite flight planning websites, Skyscanner. Typing in London to South Korean and dates either side of Yeong Ji-Won's presentation, he located two direct South Korean airline flights that aligned perfectly with the event. He reserved the flights and emailed Charlie the details with a short note:

Yeong is presenting his solution next month. We're going. Flights booked. See details below

Recently, Mike and Charlie had discussed Yeong's career after reading he would soon be launching his Smart City System. Charlie had briefly met Yeong a year earlier at a conference in Hong Kong and it was there that he had learned about the work he and his team were doing. Charlie could recall the presentation Yeong had delivered on predictive analytics and how he planned to use it in conjunction with GPS tracking. It sparked their interest at the time because conceivably, it could give their own disruption ideas an extra dimension. When Charlie opened Mike's email he smiled.

'Ah, the old boy Yeong is about to show and tell on his new system. Awesome!'

He murmured to himself, happy to also see confirmation of the recently booked flights.

'Business Class? Good chap. It's the least he can do with all the hard work I've put in recently.'

Charlie replied with a single *thump up* emoji.

'No point saying anything else. Words are for wimps, actions are for men!'

He thought, remembering Gordon Gecko's famous line from Wall Street.

While laughing at his own sense of humour, it suddenly dawned on him that life in general was about to change in so many ways. Not so much for him, but for thousands of people up and down the country. With a sense of concern triggered, he recalled almost perfectly a conversation with Mike from shortly after getting the Sand Oil and Gas news.

Do you ever think about the morals of what we are about to do? Charlie had asked.

Morals? Now that's a tricky subject. Yes of course, but that shouldn't stop us from being innovators and helping make the world a better place. At least that's how I feel about it.'

Do you think it's right to put thousands of people out of work?

We can't think about it that way. If any of our insurance company friends hit on hard times, irrespective of what we are about to do, they would not give a second thought to making thousands of people redundant. But we have a upside Charlie. Think of the millions of people who will benefit every year from what we are doing. Think of the thousands of pounds they will save by using our app, not to mention the lives that will be saved on the road as a result of drivers choosing to drive more safely because they will have a real incentive to do so. We are creating something truly revolutionary. We're using one vertical industry to horizontally disrupt an outdated and frankly expensive industry that most people think is a rip off, albeit a legal one.

But what if it was a member of your family who was about to lose their job. Charlie remembered asking.

And they found out it was your idea and your company that caused it?

In the short term they'd probably hate my guts, but none of us can be bullet-proof; shit happens. And as you know, surveys say that half of the people out there are doing jobs that wouldn't be their first choice. Disruption like this can be a silver lining in disguise, because maybe we are giving thousands of people the opportunity to make the career change that they had been thinking about for years but for one reason or another, just couldn't muster the courage to go for it. Change brings change!

You might be right. And the young kids who just spent months trying to get a job only to lose it a few months later?

That can happen at any time. It's just unfortunate timing and market forces in play. Admittedly, with this disruption we are going to drive the market for some considerable time. The industry will go through a period of turmoil but there will be survivors. People are very resourceful in the face of adversity.

Do you think others will follow our lead? Asked Charlie. He remembered pondering potential ramifications.

You know, one industry disrupting another?

Absolutely! Mike had replied.

Bear in mind that our disruption is a marriage made in heaven, so to speak. It's the perfect match. It's very hard to find two industries at opposite ends of the business spectrum that can fold into one another so well. Can you think of any others?

Coming back to the main point, do you have any scruples about what we are about to do? Charlie had pressed.

Let me think about that for a second. Okay, second over. Nah! I have no scruples at all. If it wasn't us it would be someone else. It's time to just get on and make it happen; time to disrupt a market in a way never seen before; time to unleash The Disruptor!'

Having spent time walking around that memory, Charlie's sense of fear of the unknown was being replaced mostly by excitement. He repeated those last words, *Time to unleash The Disruptor!* His mind felt easier now, continuing to raise his spirits. A silly thought to into his mind.

'Time to unleash the students!' And laughed loudly at his own sense of humour.

Chapter 17

The first of May was fast approaching. The development of the Sand Oil and Gas app had been completed, with all testing finished apart from the final usability tests in the field. To maintain secrecy, this stage would be undertaken as late as possible but not so late as to make it impossible for any problems to be addressed.

A Sand Oil filling station replica, minus the actual pumps and petrol, had been set up in the 3D office suite. Testing had been hugely informative in this environment, but it stopped short of delivering the more detailed results that could only come from actual field tests.

Charlie had recruited students with smart phones and who had access to motor vehicles for the field trials. The notices he'd distributed through the university system, had offered each participant £100 towards their studies for performing 10 tests each, spread through 1000 representative Sand Oil filling stations across the UK. The students had also been encouraged to recruit their friends and siblings at other universities, so consequently there was now a small army of eager beavers ready to complete the task. The students would not be party to the full extent of the proposition being launched but were just required to follow a few simple steps:

> *Download the Sand Oil beta app and then register.*
>
> *On the allocated test day, sequentially visit all ten of your designated Sand Oil filling stations.*
>
> *Show the filling station cashier your identity paper and inform them that you are on official Sand Oil business to field test some new software changes.*
>
> *Purchase two litres of regular unleaded petrol at any pump. When paying, quote the special pre-payment code given to you by 3D.*
>
> *Make sure you are given a till receipt which you will use to provide feedback to 3D within 24 hours, along with the results of all your tests.*
>
> *Scan the Offer Code printed on the receipt into the app or scan the bar code.*

Finally, the volunteers had to fill out a Field-Testing Sheet and upload it to the 3D website. Charlie wanted to know about smooth transactions tomorrow, but more importantly, he wanted information on any error messages or malfunctions.

The next morning, Mike awoke to the sound of a text arriving just before 7am. Just as he'd assumed, it was from Charlie announcing that he was already in the office and was ready to kick things off as planned. He was happy to read that Sand Oil were ready too, and he sent a reply:

Cool. Good Luck! See you later

Then, he reset his alarm, turned over and went back to sleep for an extra hour.

By 7:15am, the first students were calling the 3D Help Desk to confirm they were on the case. Mike and Charlie had discussed whether this might be better done through the Field Tests website but in the end they both agreed that a call to a help desk was more appropriate, and more likely to kick them into action. At least the 3D Help Desk could sense any problems early on. By half-past seven, eighty-five of the students had called, leaving just fifteen to check in.

Charlie pondered over the list of missing students - there was one missing from Newcastle, six from Manchester, two from Leeds, one from Liverpool, four from Leicester, and one from Southampton. He would deal with the two cities with most missing first, then get the desk to contact the rest.

By the time 9am came, it was only Leicester and one student from Newcastle who were still missing. Charlie asked the Help Desk to contact the first available person on the Newcastle list and offer to *double their money* if they could also perform the tests allocated to the missing student. It was a simple solution, readily accepted. By 13:00, all students had submitted their results, except for those involved in testing a group of filling stations in Newcastle, and one in Leicester.

A little later, Mike arrived with lunch - hot pizza, garlic bread and a range of drinks. The team broke away from their duties to help themselves. Charlie did the same, then beckoned Mike over to him to go through the preliminary findings.

The collated highlights on Charlie's laptop made interesting reading:

96 sets of results submitted. 4 not started.

2 sets of results with questionable quality, indicating the need for a retest.

In general, the app was performing well with no major issues in areas with good connectivity. When the app couldn't be used, the main problem would seem to be an incompatibility with older OS versions across both Android and iOS

Plymouth reported that none of the filling stations were generating the offer code or a corresponding bar code. This turned out to be a glitch from Sand Oil, who confirmed they hadn't yet successfully completed the latest software upgrade of that filling station. They promised to schedule completion for that week and would double-check their records for any others that might have been missed. Both men felt relieved at the mostly successful results.

'And Charlie, did your guys turn on the Customer Notifications during the testing?'

'Only in test mode. None of the students got any of the notifications but we logged everything from the app. One thing we need to do next time is emphasise to our student rent a crowd that speeding between filling stations is not permitted.'

'Do I need to do anything or are we good for the day?' Mike checked.

'Nah Mike, I think we're good. I'll just contact the Sand Oil operatives to thank them for their support and ask them to confirm their plans over the next day or so. Then, it's debriefing the students tomorrow, and after we've brought the few missed stations up to date, we'll be all set for the full launch on first of May.'

'And we've paid these guys?'

'Yeah, as soon as each student submitting their results had them accepted, a payment was automatically generated.'

'Great job Charlie. Great work from the whole team, and dare I say it, great work from the student community. That's gone a whole lot smoother than I anticipated. See you later.'

The final task of the day for Charlie was to contact Sand Oil Central Operations, to advise them of the results and confirm any next steps. Mike had already left. As he walked out of the building, he could feel the cool April evening on his face. Taking in some of that fresh air and looking around, he noticed a car parked side-on, with someone still behind the wheel. He recognised the driver but tried not to make his interest too obvious.

'Why on earth is Lenny Tall sat in a car outside our building?'

As Mike started to walk towards the car, he could see Lenny sink into his seat hoping not to be spotted. Then he gunned the engine and, without headlights, sped past Mike. Bemused, he scratched his chin and continued towards his own car.

'Why was Lenny Tall spying on 3D's offices?' Mike asked himself, shaking and now scratching his head. But as he walked to his car, he couldn't shake off the idea of there being something more sinister in Lenny Tall's actions.

'Perhaps,' thought Mike, 'he was trying to unearth more than what was already agreed?'

He knew Lenny was the type of guy who would go to any length to reach his goals.

'But why stake out our office?'

This whole thing was still too puzzling for Mike. He'd forget about it for now but was sure Lenny Tall had just committed a breach of their contract.

'Maybe it was a sign of things to come?' he concluded.

Lenny Tall's career was well on its in being disrupted! Only he didn't know it yet!

The Disruption Begins

Chapter 18

The day Andrew Dodd was dreading had finally arrived. After checking one last time for a better car insurance quote, he was still frustrated and didn't know which way to turn. Was it to be a lower premium with a bigger excess or a bigger premium and a lower excess? Both scenarios were equally unpalatable. On top of his list of frustrations, his wife, Kate, had gone ahead and arranged an appointment with Gloria, her sister. He hated the idea of giving Gloria his business for a year, but he respected his wife's wishes to at least ask Gloria for a quote. His mood was one of reluctant compliance.

Kate was up early, dressed and ready for the trip to Dorchester. Andrew was dragging his heels, hoping for a lesser sentence than an hour with Gloria.

'Oh, do get ready darling, Gloria is expecting us at ten. I spoke with her last night. Said she's looking forward to seeing us, it's been a while.' Kate was doing her best to rally her husband.

'Coming darling - I was just checking the traffic news' Andrew offered as an excuse to delay or if possible, postpone the trip indefinitely. 'Have you seen my driving shoes?' As he looked glum-eyed at Kate.

'I know why you are doing this; time to snap out of it. We have forty-five minutes to get to Dorchester, park up and walk over to my sister's shop. I want to be having morning tea promptly at eleven, then spend a delightful couple of hours looking around the shops; two sisters enjoying time together. Now get a move on!'

'Sister, tea, sister, shops - here we go again. A simple trip for an insurance quote turns out to be a major blinking social event and as usual, I'll be stuck in the middle of it, with words going in one ear and straight out the other, with no comprehension in between.' Andrew couldn't see the point of dragging him along. The online insurance quotes were looking extra attractive now.

'Darling, you know very well that you don't have any driving shoes. You drive in any pair of shoes, now stop stalling and let's get going!'

Within five minutes they were on the road, hurtling (below the speed limit), towards *Gloriaville*.

Andrew chuckled to himself and quietly murmured.

'I like that'.

For him, Dorchester was always *Gloriaville,* but it could even be *GloriaVile* for him on occasions. He couldn't contain himself any longer and burst out laughing.

'Why are you laughing?'

'Nothing darling, just laughing at why I thought I had "driving shoes!"'

Approaching ten, they pulled into the Lower Car Park in Gloriaville, Dorchester.

'Hurry up. I can't remember the last time you took two wrong turnings on such a familiar route!'

At 10am. sharp they arrived outside Gloria's shop, stopping for a moment to catch their breath.

Across the top of the entrance door was emblazoned;

Voted Independent Car Insurance Broker of the Year. Proprietor: Gloria Stenson.

'Kate, my lovely sister Kate, I've missed you!' Both ladies embraced like missing war children.

'You haven't changed Andrew; still that strong sturdy look of a man with intentions!'

Andrew knew his intentions well - to turn around and run!

'Come in, come in,' screamed Gloria, high-pitched and unprofessional. 'How are you both? New shoes Andrew, a new jumper and a new shirt, you do look the country gentleman,' she expressed, with gushing enthusiasm.

'My beautiful sister, always the most-kind words,' acknowledged Kate.

'Sit down, sit down, sit down! Take the weight off those shoes Andrew.'

Andrew bloody hated Gloria. She had a personality somewhere between Mrs Hyacinth Bouquet and Minnie Mouse, which just ate away at him in the most tedious of ways, but for Kate's sake he would play along.

'Thankyou Gloria. You're always so kind and as bright as the day is long. How's Minnie Mouse?'

Thank fully neither heard him. They were too busy talking at each other, over each other, under each other and through each other. If it had been two guys in conversation, even after five minutes, punches would have been thrown. He wasn't going to mention car insurance but would do everything he could to keep it social, not business. He wanted to avoid the social as well. It was a small price to pay for avoiding any discussion on cars!

While the conversation flowed like a torrent, and in and out of Andrew's ears just as he had predicted, Gloria printed off a quote for Andrew to read. Without a break in conversation, she slid it over to him and continued her banter with Kate. Andrew scanned the quote, noting the ten-percent discount for loyalty, and another for family.

'In a lot of cases, a twenty-percent discount would seem quite reasonable,' he thought to himself as his eyes wandered up and down the paper looking for the catch. He reflected further and recalled the quotes produced by MoneySuperMarket and GoCompare earlier that morning. Even with the twin discounts, Gloria's quote wasn't any cheaper, and certainly not worth his agreeing there and then.

After pondering for a moment, he broke into the two-way talk, stunning both women into silence.

'Thank you for the quote, Gloria. After careful reflection and comparison with other quotes I've obtained, it's too expensive. Now without any further ado, I'll leave you two ladies to talk.'

Twenty-two minutes after arriving, he'd had enough. He felt marginalised by the conversation and completely disinterested in anything else that might come to the fore in the next half-hour. After silencing the two women with his uncharacteristic outburst, he stood up turned on his heels, and with perfect precision, left the shop. In his mind it was a moment of triumph. Gloria treated it as if her brother-in-law didn't care about her and burst into tears. Kate, on the other hand, spent the next hour making excuses and trying to calm her down before the next client arrived.

But Andrew didn't care - he was right. Gloria was too expensive and that was that! One day he would probably have to apologise but for now The Fox and Hounds was his destination for a small celebratory drink or two.

Shortly before two o'clock, Kate entered the pub looking rather scornful.

'There you are! And a fine brother-in-law you've been today,' as she scorned Andrew for his earlier behaviour.

The regular pub clientele listened discretely, ready to take evasive action if it came to blows.

'Yeah well, handling delicate matters was never my forte. Point is, your sister's car insurance quote was amongst the highest I'd obtained. Business is business - we can't afford her. I'll just go online like before and renew the car insurance at the best value-for-money price I can get.'

There was an element of Dutch courage in his stand against Kate. Still scolding him for the trouble he had caused, she conceded he was usually right in such matters.

'Okay, time to go. I'll drive because you've evidently had one too many,' she said, reaching out her open hand for the keys.

After two very enjoyable pints of smooth bitter, a chat with the pub locals and a telling off from his wife, Andrew spent an awkward evening at home. After sleeping off some of his beer, Andrew declared he was going to bed because we wanted to be up early in the morning to finalise renewing his car insurance. He was also keen to avoid any further sparks flying between he and Kate. Whilst he was right about the cost of Gloria's quote, he admitted he had celebrated rather too well, after leaving Kate to console poor Gloria.

The month of May dawned, and Andrew Dodd, armed with his keenly fought freedom of choice and now invalid insurance certificate, must immediately see about purchasing car insurance for the year. Otherwise he would not be able to drive his car or protect it on the driveway. He briefly recalled the previous uncomfortable day in Dorchester and how he ended all discussion with – There are better deals on the internet and that's where I'm going, although he couldn't remember the words exactly.

Kate was also up early, busily preparing breakfast in the kitchen.

Andrew switched on his computer and after a couple of minutes, clicked on his browser to show Google. He entered *low cost car insurance* and waited patiently for a response.

As usual, there was a long list of results, so he started to scroll down the page. He glanced over GoCompare, MoneySuperMarket, Confused and many more of the usual car insurers. Then a news article caught his eye from a television media company called TechWatch;

> *TechWatch Exclusive! Get free car insurance every time you fill up!*

He clicked on the link provided, which took him to the website;

> *www.SandOilInsurance.com.*

Then he read the headline;

> *Free comprehensive car insurance every time your car is filled with our fuel - petrol or diesel.*
>
> *Sand Oil Insurance, a wholly owned subsidiary of Sand Oil and Gas, is pleased to announce a new way to insure your car. Fill your car tank up at any of our filling station outlets and your vehicle will be automatically insured by us. No more costly insurance premiums! No more trying to find cost effective cover and no more discrimination on age, experience or your job as a driver. This is probably the best car insurance deal you will ever get.*

Andrew read it again. He stopped and in disbelief shouted out to his wife.

'Kate come, come and see this! Kate, come now!' his excitement getting the better of him. When Kate hurried in, drying her hands on a towel, he pointed to the screen.

'Read that page. Am I reading it correctly or have I missed something?'

Kate studied the page.

'Fill your car up with our fuel and we'll cover you with comprehensive car insurance for as long as you continue to do so.'

'I was right. That's what I read too,' Andrew concluded.

'I just take my car down to the local Sand Oil filling station and buy their fuel?'

'Not quite darling,' said Kate. 'You have to download the Sand Oil app, register and then you can take advantage of this deal. Look, there's a help guide on one of the other pages.'

Andrew clicked through and read the details.

'It looks very simple; just do as they say and make sure I keep the receipt. It will have an eight-digit code or a bar code printed on it. All I need to do is open the app and scan the bar code, which confirms the petrol as Sand Oil and Bob's your uncle, the car is insured. It's genius. I always have to buy petrol anyway, so why not from Sand Oil?'

'There's bound to be a catch darling, so read the small print before you spend any money,' Kate advised as she returned to the kitchen.

After ten minutes, Andrew had followed all the instructions, carefully reading the Terms and

Conditions, word by word, line by line. All the usual conditions were present. He read out the list:

'Driving while under the influence of drugs; driving whilst under the influence of alcohol; reckless driving; driving whilst severely distracted i.e. engaging in a sexual practice; driving in excess of the speed limit,' and so on.

Towards the end of the Terms and Conditions, he came to a section that he was certain had not been part of any previous policy. It was called *Customer Notifications.*

'What can these be?', he thought to himself. Reading on through the details, he made a mental note to check that his phone's voice activation was ON, so he could hear any notifications whilst remaining safe and legal on the road.

After reading through this final section, Andrew clicked on the radio button to accept. He was more than happy, and especially liked the part about Warning Notifications. He regarded himself as a good driver and resented that fact the premiums had been increasing year on year to help insurance companies offset the risks of bad driving. He was fed up of paying for bad drivers to be on the road and very much liked the idea of monitoring and helping improve their behaviour through an app.

He closed his laptop and went into the kitchen.

'Darling, I am going to do this! I'm going to insure the car and get free petrol. No! I mean I'm going to fill the car up with petrol and get free car insurance.' They both giggled.

Just yesterday, he had been facing a sizeable increase in his insurance premium. Now, on this first day of May, all he needed to do was fill up his car at a Sand Oil filling station, pay and then scan a bar code into the app.

'At last,' he said, 'an oil company that cares about its customers.'

The eager customer set off for the nearest Sand Oil filling station. The roads were quiet. On arrival, he was surprised not to find queues around the block. The filling station forecourt was empty. He started to doubt the authenticity of the Sand Oil Insurance website.

Nonetheless, he filled up his car then went to the kiosk to hand over his debit card to a cashier.

'Sir, would you like to take advantage of our special offer of comprehensive car insurance?'

Andrew stuttered briefly, and almost embarrassed replied emphatically,

'Yes please!'

'Do you have a smartphone with you sir, that already has the Sand Oil App installed?' the attended asked.

He did and handed the phone to the cashier who opened the app and scanned the bar code showing on the printed receipt.

'There you go sir. You and your car are now comprehensively insured, and as long as you continue to fill up with Sand Oil fuel, this will continue to be the case,' she said, handing back his phone.

Andrew noted the new message on his screen, then the voice of a computer robot reading it aloud;

> *Advisory: Congratulations Mr. Dodd you are our very first customer. Welcome to Sand Oil Insurance and a world of new possibilities. Happy driving and be safe out there.*

'Wow!' exclaimed Andrew,
'I'm the first. No wonder there were no queues, I'm the first.'

It was still very early in the morning with hardly anyone about, as he gazed out through the filling station window before walking back to his car. Having irresponsibly left buying insurance until his last certificate had expired, he'd risen early to sort it out, and at only a few minutes past 7am, it was done. This was one of the best starts to a day he could ever remember! By the time he was turning the ignition, four of the six pumps were in action.

'I wonder,' he thought, 'are these folks aware of Sand Oil Insurance?'

He didn't give it any more thought and slowly drove off. Whilst passing through the urban streets he noticed he was being even more careful in his driving, remembering what would happen if he got one of those Sand Oil Insurance Warning Notifications. He wasn't going to take any risks and lose the deal of the century. Extremely happy with his day's work thus far, a very large satisfied smile spread across his face, from cheek to cheek. He was looking forward to breakfast now and spending the day in the garden with Kate. Suddenly he felt very hungry.

'If only managing the garden was as easy as arranging car insurance,' he thought, quickly followed by 'I wonder how this will affect GloriaVile?'

He instantly felt guilty over his previous day's behaviour.

'Anyway, she was still too expensive, based on what I've been quoted elsewhere', he shrugged. 'But this new Sand Oil Insurance approach will surely make it impossible for Gloria to sell anymore car insurance.'

For a moment, he felt very sorry for his sister-in-law. He didn't think it possible; his guilt went deeper.

Chapter 19

As the morning moved on, the TechWatch TV Studio continued to provided coverage of the breaking story. They received hundreds of enquires from members of the public and other media companies, all trying to get more information.

The producer remained tight-lipped, as did the rest of the show's crew, except one Lenny Tall who decided the time was right to hold his own live coverage from the steps of the 3D office building. Word reached Mike and Charlie who were locked in their office bunker ensuring all was progressing well with the launch.
'So that's why he was parked outside our offices,' he remembered to Charlie. 'I saw him a few weeks ago, lurking around outside. It seems Mr. Tall was working out where to hold his very own live broadcast. It's a pity he didn't keep to the contract. Now we'll just have to give his bosses a call and shout breach! And all the evidence we need is going out live on TV - nice one Lenny', said Mike, sarcastically.
Mike and Charlie weren't particularly bothered by the broadcast; in fact, it fitted in quite well with the overall publicity of the day, but from here Lenny Tall would find himself in a predicament and would have to face the consequences.
Enjoying the excitement of this real-life entrapment, Adam Barth seized the moment to

explain the app's in-built security in its entirety to Mike, and fill Charlie in on the latest iterations.

'Basically, I've built a castle structure inside the app. There's an outer wall with four towers, an inner wall and a draw bridge with a moat and keep.'

Mike scratched his head, while Charlie glowed with pride at the kid, and Adam went deeper.

'All security, and for that matter, all information security, was born out of the defences used in a castle to keep unwanted guests or invaders out. All I've done is create it in software code and the rest of the team have integrated it into the app.'

'Sounds brilliant,' said Mike, still puzzling, 'but why?'

'Hackers will quickly hear about this app because it's in the news, then they will try to break into it to steal data; either customer data or user data. They'll do this for two reasons, 1) Because they can sell the information they steal on the black market and 2) they can then claim notoriety for having hacked the app. Either way, if it's proved the app has been hacked, then its game over for Sand Oil and 3D. No-one will trust the app, Sand Oil will sue, and 3D will spend all its hard-earned cash trying to dig itself out of a very big hole.'

There were sharp intakes of breath from both founders, as they pondered the potential repercussions, then Charlie was eager to chip in, 'Tell him about the game!'

'Okay. First let me tell you that it would be very difficult to hack this app, if at all. A hacker would need to have a sophisticated array of tools and computing power to break the encryption algorithms. Anyway, that won't stop someone trying, so just to give us a little bit of insurance, I've laid a few paths for a hacker to follow. Once a hacker finds his way into the castle (or rather, the outer security wall of the app), then the same hacker is deemed to be inside Room 1. The app will take the hacker on a simple journey making it look like he's getting further and further into the castle and towards the keep (our data), when in fact he's being systematically and game-fully given the run around at the outer walls. He won't be able to go forward or backwards, unless we let him, and he certainly won't be able to go from the outer wall to the inner wall and from there, onto the keep. In short we have him by the hacker balls!'

Charlie and Mike were amazed to hear about the elaborate game and the trap security, but Mike was still puzzled, so asked some more questions.

Adam explained, 'Once a hacker has stolen data, published it on the dark web and claimed success, there's no incentive for other hacker will bother, so thereon in, the app will be left alone!'

'So, if a hacker publishes something on the dark web, it will be correctly assumed by public and authorities alike that the app has been hacked, and so be brought into disrepute?'

'That really depends on what the hacker publishes. Trust me, the app is safe and secure. It won't attract any adverse publicity. A hacker can only publish what he finds and will only release the information to those who pay him.'

Mike took Charlie to one side.

'This lad is brilliant, but there's something about him and this worries me. Can you do a bit of digging around to try to find out more about him and his background? Something's not quite right here. I admire his work and the castle design is amazing, but he's almost too good to be true and he's certainly too good to be picked up at random from a university class. We're talking one in a million and those odds make me highly suspicious. What if he's a plant?'

Mike went back to studying the latest app download figures and read comments on social media. 'And by the way, I'm making a little trip this afternoon so will be out of the office the rest of the day.'

Now Charlie wished he'd come clean at the time and told Mike that Adam was Jo's son. 'Come to think of it,' he quietly realised, 'why is Adam's accent is so different to Jo's?' He would ask Jo later, but for now he needed to get the 3D team started on extracting data and loading it into his analytical tools. Progress reports and analytics had been promised to Sand Oil, and these had to be delivered to Mike in time for the first formal update.

Chapter 20

The Operations Director at Insurance Direct called John Calcott.

'Sir, all our call centres have gone unusually quiet. We're at about fifty-percent of what we would normally expect for this time of day. I've declared a major incident whilst we investigate the cause, in case it's some sort of virus attack. IT tells me everything is up and running, and as far as they can tell from their monitoring screens, all services, internal and external, are available.'

Calcott asked the usual questions about major events on TV, if anything was going on around the world that might distract people, and each time the answer was a confident *no*!

'Call me in an hour with an update.' The CEO commanded.

The CEO of possibly the largest insurance company in Europe, logged into his computer and began searching Google. There were multiple reports detailing the announcement from Sand Oil and Gas about their app. He then opened a new tab for Twitter to find out what was trending. "Free car insurance app" was at the top, followed by the usual blend of tweets and gossip about celebrities.

He called his Social Media Director.

'In the next hour, I need a comprehensive report from across all our social media channels and, specifically, any mention of free car insurance, Sand

Oil and Gas or a company called 3D. I also need to know what our customers are saying about it and what they are saying about us.' The Social Media Director immediately began pulling data from all the main socials, in readiness to report back within the hour.

Across the city, Frank Delaney was having a similar conversation with his Operations Director. The feedback was very positive. All social media channels were *buzzing with excitement,* and all filling station outlets had reported their busiest day since the oil crisis back in the 1970s. Long queues had been reported at pretty much every station they owned. The situation was currently under control.

Frank gave a smile and thanked his Operations Director. 'Good that I gave the go ahead to ensure that every filling station was ready for the increase in demand. Can you get in touch with Distribution and ensure they are ready to despatch new supplies as soon as stations start reporting 50% capacity? It'll take time to mobilise and whilst some people might think this is a short-term gimmick to sell more fuel, we need to ensure we don't give anybody any reason to doubt our intentions. This is the deal of the century and we must be prepared to maintain supplies at all costs. We must ride out the peak and give it time for demand to settle down to a more "predicable" pattern.

The Operations Director agreed and congratulated Frank on his vision. It was only the first day and already the impact of their tiny little app was being widely felt across the country.

Chapter 21

'Mum! Dad! I've found car insurance!' yelled Chris Reid to his parents with unrestrained excitement. 'There's this new app and all you have to do is fill your car up with their petrol and you're insured. I can pay as I go! Unbelievable! I love it!'

Like many his age, Chris was impetuous. He'd taken his driving test three times and failed twice. He was told on the two failed attempts that he had been travelling too fast and was failed on the spot both times in under five minutes.

His parents had bought him a car for his eighteenth birthday, and he could drive on the condition that he obtained comprehensive car insurance and promised them he would slow down. He agreed of course, but he couldn't wait to get out on the open roads, country lanes and the motorway to let rip. Speed was his motivation for learning to drive and getting a car. He pleaded with his parents for a car and eventually they relented. They bought him a small engine three-door that could do 90mph as a top speed but took a decade to get to 60. In their minds, it was one way to control his "greed for speed".

Chris downloaded the app, registered and ticked the Ts and Cs box but without reading any of the terms (he'd do that later, he told himself). His dad drove him over to the local Sand Oil filling station.

After an hour long wait, the tank was finally full. The teen entered the code and received confirmation that he was comprehensively insured and ready to go. His dad agreed to walk back and leave Chris free to roam.

Out on the road again, the new driver stopped to talk with friends and to show off his car and the new app. He noticed the app message box flashing but ignored it; he was too excited driving his own car at last. He bragged about the 70mph he achieved on one of the back roads, and how he had taken it screeching around tight corners.

'Man! It was awesome! I must have been on two wheels at one stage!'

His friends told him to go easy. It was his first time out on the open roads alone and he still needed to find his feet. He nodded, 'Yeah, yeah! I'll go easy. I'll take my speed down to 69mph,' and laughed. He turned the key in the ignition and sped off to the sound of his friends hollering, 'Slow down!'.

Stopped at traffic lights, he noticed the app message count had gone up to three. He decided to look later because for now, he was just enjoying the freedom of driving – at speed! By 5pm, the app message count had gone up to eight, and the funny round box circling the number six had turned red.

'Perhaps it's time to go home for tea and tell mum and dad about my day - leaving out my racing, of course.'

But all the driving and excitement had made him thirsty as well as hungry. He stopped at a country pub for a beer and a bag of crisps. Before long, he was back in the car ready for the next stage of the circuit, or so he called it. It started to rain; first time in a few days. On the far side of the next village, the car left the road and hit a tree. It was a notorious blackspot with lots of warning signs. Chris was killed instantly.

When the police arrived at the scene, it was obvious that a tragedy had occurred; small car, young person. They'd seen it many times before. The skid marks were still evident, even on the rain-soaked road. A large wedge of soil from an earthen bank had been ploughed and splattered over the scene, mostly across the front of the car. The car had hit the raised bank, carved out the top section and then continued into the tree.

Chris's parents were watching a TV quiz show and preparing tea when the doorbell rang. His dad opened the door, knowing immediately that something was wrong.
'Mr. Reid?' the police officer asked.
'Yes, what's happened? Is it Chris? Oh my God, it's got to be Chris?'

Chapter 22

It was almost closing time when a potential new client entered Gloria Stenson's shop.

'Hello, my name is Mike Day. I was reading about your achievements and wanted to meet you in person. Congratulations on your new award. You must be very proud of your achievements?'

Gloria was taken aback. She had been so busy lately that she was blissfully unaware she had won the award again as *Independent Car Insurance Broker of the Year.*

Gloria nodded, 'Come in Mr. Day. Thank you for the news! Yes, that's right, I've been in the car insurance business for over thirty-five years and have very many satisfied customers.'

'Pleased to meet you Ms. Stenson,' as they both shook hands. Gloria reciprocated.

'Tea or coffee Mr. Day?'

'Black coffee please. Thank you.'

Gloria fixed two coffees and returned to her desk.

'What can I do for you Mr. Day?' she enquired.

'Well, it's more of a question of what I can do for you Ms. Stenson.'

'I see - or rather I don't see,' she replied, smiling.

Mike started to explain the background to Sand Oil Insurance and how it was now offering free comprehensive car insurance through a specially developed app.

'What utter rubbish you speak Mr. Day! That's just fake news like lots of other stories you hear about on the internet. I dismissed it in an instant, as soon as I saw it, as a silly joke!'

'I assure you Ms. Stenson – it's not joke,' Mike said with his most serious tone.

'Give me a minute Mr. Day, as I check this out.'

Gloria opened her laptop and Google-searched for Sand Oil Insurance. Several references appeared but the most prominent one was on *BBC News* – a site Gloria trusted. The most recent article was dated 1 May, timed at 15:00, and it read:

> *Breaking News: Giant Sand Oil and Gas affirms launch of app offering customers free comprehensive car insurance.*

She went back to Google and clicked on Sky News. Their headline read:

> *Drive up, drive up and fill up for free car insurance. A radical new way to pay for car insurance has been unveiled by Sand Oil, through a new subsidiary called Sand Oil Insurance. Launched early this morning, the reaction from consumers has been unprecedented. It's even been reported that taxi drivers have been cancelling their hugely expensive policies in favour of using the new app.*

'Okay Mr. Day, you have my attention. If this is true, and by all accounts it looks that way, I'm out of business!' There was a terse tone to her voice.

'Ms. Stenson, it's only a matter of time before all your customers or clients or whatever you call them switch over to Sand Oil Insurance. The consequences of this are obvious. You will never be able to sell another car policy, if someone has access to a smartphone and uses this app. Consider the alternatives; what would you do? Continue paying £500 or £600 for a policy that you can now get for free? Not even the dumbest of the dumb would do that.'

'But why are you here? I hope not to gloat Mr. Day?'

Mike explained.

'Working with Sand Oil and Gas, it was my company that developed the app and formed a business partnership with them. During my research into the oil and insurance industries, I came across your name. You're well regarded locally and from what I've read, you have given great service to both the industry and your customers over many years. In a few cases, I hear that you have actually paid the client's insurance costs yourself, which, if I might say, is a very generous and caring act to those struggling to keep their cars on the road. You're the best of the best and for that reason I want to offer you a position in my company, 3D.'

'A position?'

Gloria exclaimed with both shock and indignation.

'You come here out of nowhere, tell me I can't sell car insurance anymore, pamper me with some nice words and now you want to offer me a job?'

'Yes.'

'Mr. Day, I'm sure you have your reasons for doing what you are doing to the car insurance industry (God only knows it needed a bit of shake up), but after spending most of my working life within an industry I love, there's no way I can just switch over to doing something else. I know I can't beat you, but sure as hell I'm not going to join you.'

Mike took a deep breath. Perhaps he was wrong to make such an offer. He had certainly underestimated the venom of Gloria's response.

'At least her venom wasn't poisonous,' he considered.

After recomposing herself, she continued with all guns blazing.

'Mr. Day, I thank you for your offer but no thanks. I will take my chances and do what I need to do to keep my business running. Good day sir.'

Gloria was already at the door holding it wide open for Mike to crawl through.

'You are a smart woman and I apologise that by coming here I may have offended you or taken a liberty. My intentions were sincere, if just poorly thought through. I wish you every success in whatever you decide to do. Thank you for your time.'

Gloria somehow managed to open the door wider. The hinges creaked under the pressure. She was angry now. The news she had just received began to sink in and she was desperate to see the back of this man. As soon as Mike was across the threshold of the shop, the door was forcefully closed behind him.

Returning to her desk with tears in her eyes, she trembled.

'What am I going to do?'

There was absolutely no way she could compete with an offer of free car insurance. She concluded.

'No-one in the entire motor insurance industry can compete with free car insurance. This industry is dead in the water. I'm part of the industry therefore my company is dead.'

She paused before a final cry.

'What on earth am I going to do?'

After the Disruption

Chapter 23

A week after the launch, all was going well. The initial media hype had died down, new downloads and registrations continued to beat all expectations, and the much-anticipated trip to the Far East had arrived. After eating, Mike and Charlie settled down to watch their own choices of inflight movie. They shot each other the occasional look but said very little, as both were very tired.

After fourteen hours, the flight finally touched down at Seoul Incheon Airport, jolting them awake as the aircraft hit the runway and the engines were thrown into reverse. After clearing immigration, the hotel was only a short taxi ride away. They didn't have much time, so decided to go straight to the hotel, grab a quick shower and change of clothes, before continuing onto the Chihye Electronics Conference. They made it just in time and congratulated themselves for their precise timing; London to Seoul, and into theirs seats with two minutes to spare.

Yeong Ji-Won was standing in the wings of the auditorium, feeling slightly nervous but ready to unveil his "Soul of the City Vision". It was not his intention to talk extensively. Instead, he was adamant that demonstrating elements of his City Vision through role play was the best form of illustration. He would narrate, while everyone else would act out their parts in the scenes to come.

The CEO of Chihye Electronics, the second largest electronics company in South Korea, prepared to introduce Yeong Ji-Won to the waiting media, partner companies and invited guests. The auditorium was full. The Soul of the City Vision was to be hailed as a revolution in city management, a revolution much needed in South Korea, never mind the rest of the world.

Mike and Charlie sat back in their chairs and awaited the on-stage arrival of Yeong Ji-Won. They recalled reading about Yeong's work during the last year and had been engaged enough to prioritise being here for the unveiling. And who knew, potentially they could be first in line to integrate elements of the Soul of the City Vision with a partner app, their Sand Oil app, and distribute the synergistic use of this technology across the UK and perhaps, mainland Europe too. They didn't know exactly what Yeong was going to unveil, but if the rumours were true, he might just have the answer to one of European cities' biggest challenges – traffic congestion. Mike and Charlie had discussed this issue several times, even having considered incorporating advanced, big data analytics within the app, but development time proved too short and besides, Yeong was rumoured to be already much further down the path they hoped to tread. Before they could decide one way or the other, they needed to listen to Mr. Yeong, as he introduced his vision.

The lights dimmed, and the man of the moment emerged, taking his position centre stage. Behind him, just dark, empty space. He started to speak.

> *Ladies and gentlemen, what I am about to present to you is the culmination of three years of research and development from myself and hundreds of smart people, some even smarter than me.*

There were a few laughs.

> *But first, I want to remind you of the "BIG 10" problems we were trying to solve.*

In the background a large screen lit up, with words slowly scrolling upwards. He began by calling out each of the problems and quoting the related statistics each time.

> *Traffic Congestion, Air Pollution, Infrastructure Maintenance, Overcrowding, Security Threats, Unemployment in Young People, Effects of Global Warming, Environmental Conservation, Costly Public Transport, Population Growth and finally - Inaction! For the geniuses amongst you, you're right, you did count eleven. But number eleven is not one of the problems we seek to address. It only becomes a problem if we don't act!*

The auditorium was silent. Mike and Charlie gave each other a quick glance, confirming their mutual interest.

Following the Big 10 slides, the term *Traffic Congestion* in oversized letters, returned to the screen once more. Yeong continued with examples and statistics, before coming to an abrupt stop. He waited, thrilling in the power of silence all around.

Mike and Charlie found themselves leaning forward and listening carefully, watching the story unfold on the screen behind the speaker. Mike scanned the room. It was the same at every level – everyone was captivated by Yeong and his story. Cities across the world struggle with congestion, CO_2 emissions and poor air quality, exacerbated by ineffective traffic flow. And even now, not every car had an automatic idle switch.

> *Ladies and gentlemen, in setting out to solve these problems, we concluded it was better to look at the bigger picture and ask ourselves "why" traffic lights, were invented in the first place.*

After explaining why, he paused once more.

> *Today, the main issue is a simple case of supply and demand. Too much demand for road capacity and not enough road capacity available during the busiest times of the day.*

> *These days, it's getting harder to work out when rush hour starts and when it finishes. Our roads are getting busier and busier every day, and as the numbers increase so do air-polluting particulates, CO, SO2, NOx, and the global warming greenhouse gas, CO2. The strain continues to impact the underlying infrastructure, and we haven't even touched on public transport yet.*

Yeong hesitated to glance around the auditorium. He could see that everyone was still hooked, gazing eagerly in his direction.

> *Ladies and gentlemen, at Chihye Electronics we believe there is just one solution to this problem of congestion. Layering solution after solution on top of problem after problem, only makes an increasingly complex situation, incrementally more difficult to solve.*

> *The Soul of the City Vision is not about the soul of the city, per se; It's about life. More specifically a work-life balance. Every day I see people in cars travelling across this city and every day, I see the same old problems. At Chihye Electronics we want to introduce you to the EcoPodOffice™ the world's most advanced, connected and most technologically progressive working environment on the planet. Why travel to work, when work can travel to you?*

From their elevated position, Mike and Charlie could see the stage floor opening. Rising from the centre came an amazing, futuristic-looking pod-like object. The entrepreneur started to explain the thinking behind the EcoPodOffice™.

The EcoPodOffice™ is the complete working environment.

He reeled off its features.

Each one is solar-powered and air-conditioned. With ergonomically designed seating, you'll find desk space for three people, high and low storage, two of the latest design Ultra Slim TV screens - one for keeping abreast of news, the other for conference calls.

The pods were fibre optic connected, with immersive technology headsets, and a completely secure front door and two windows.

The EcoPodOffice™,' Yeong continued, 'comes with free installation, free internet and free power. All we ask is that you pay one USD per day for maintenance. It comes with a simple "tap and pay" terminal and there are several category variations; private, public, utility and modular. The EcoPodOffice™ can be installed at home, in the garden, a bar or in specially designated civic "eco" areas.

He then gave his views on how to solve the problem of congestion.

> *It's not a case of opting for more cars because they just increase emissions. Globally, we need less vehicles on the road emitting poisonous gases and particulates, which as a result will reduce the need for intensive traffic management. The more people work from home or closer to home, the less need there is for travel, and by extension, there will be less time people are being unproductive, sitting in cars, busy doing nothing.*

Yeong took a longer pause now, hearing a steady but growing round of applause. The whole auditorium erupted with cheers and whistles. Yeong had landed the EcoPodOffice™ and it was a sensation.

The two Brit's looked at each other, both with the same thought. They hadn't considered anything like the EcoPodOffice™ as an aid to congestion and traffic management. The idea was as radical, as it was simple. With modern connective technology improving almost daily, a larger proportion of the workforce would not have to make journeys to get to their desks. Why shouldn't more people work from home? Many already did, and not just those who run their own small businesses. It was a complete technology solution for many growing problems and would still give people a sense of going to work each day but for a fraction of the cost and time. If one million people worked from an EcoPodOffice™, the city would benefit from significantly less congestion, less carbon emissions, cleaner air and less physical stress on the road infrastructure.

Yeong asked delegates if they had any questions before breaking for lunch. Several waving arms shot up from people eager to know about the size of the EcoPodOffice ™, its weight and how long it would take to manufacture, distribute and install. Patiently, one by one, Yeong answered everyone, with the biggest surprise for all being that each pod comes in a series of self-build flat packs weighing less than 200 kilos. Trials with members of the public who enjoyed DIY showed that it could take an average of two hours to erect and another fifteen minutes to become fully connected. EcoPodOffice™ was an eco-friendly office in a box.

Chapter 24

Gloria Stenson was getting ready for lunch. She had just one afternoon appointment which was scheduled for 3pm. In the two weeks since the launch of the Sand Oil app, appointments had almost completely disappeared from her schedule. Her once loyal customers had vanished without a trace.

'I've loads of time,' she thought, 'I'll call Beth and we can discuss this oil company.'

Beth was Gloria's oldest friend. They'd known each other for several years, and she was one of the few people she trusted with her problems. Gloria valued her advice, or the lack of it most of the time. Beth was Gloria's friendly therapist, or so it seemed over the years.

Just before one o'clock, Gloria locked the shop and walked with purpose towards the Dorchester Tea Rooms. The short walk was enough time to allow her to relax and think about what she would have to eat.

She saw Beth arriving just before her and called out, 'Woo-hoo, Beth!'

Hearing her name, Beth turned to greet her friend. 'Good afternoon Gloria, are you hungry? I'm starved. Let's find our table and order before I burn another calorie.' Beth loved her food and in one swoop, off-loaded her coat, landed in her chair and managed to open the menu at the precise page she wanted.

'I don't know why you even look at the menu Beth because you always have the same thing,' stated Gloria.

'Well Gloria, it's like this, you never know if there's going to be something different or delightful that I might prefer to my usual order,' she replied. 'Now tell me about this oil company and this "app" thing. What is an app my dear?'

'That's it,' thought Gloria as she pulled her chair in. 'I'll do something different and delightful. You are a genius Beth. I haven't even given you any details about my problem and you've already helped me determine how I might find a solution. If you didn't know it already, Beth you're a genius.'

'What's that about a genius dear? Did you say something important?' asked Beth, who was deep in thought, scouring the menu for something *delightful and different.*

As the waitress approached, Beth jumped in.

'My usual please Anna.' Leaning towards Gloria, the waitress opened her writing pad to show what she had written;

Beth – My usual (Quiche Lorraine, a small side salad, with English tea and scones to follow).

They both giggled.
'What would you like Ms. Stenson?' Anna asked.
'I'd like something different and delightful,' Gloria replied with a warm smile.

'Thank you,' she acknowledged. 'I'll bring you the special of the day with English tea and a slice of hot chocolate cake.' And with that, she left to place the order at the kitchen.

Waiting for their lunch, the two old friends embarked on a conversation about the local news and what else was new in the neighbourhood. They didn't quite get around to talking about apps or problems. Gloria now had the key to help unlock some answers, so she was half-in and out of the conversation, as she walked herself through a range of options in her imagination.

Soon, Anna brought lunch and the two ladies eased into a further all-consuming conversation, mostly driven by Beth. Seeing them both content and getting on with their food, Anna took a short break. She opened WhatsApp on her mobile and started a chat with her boyfriend in Romania.

'Da!' was the prompt response. Anna typed further.

'You should use English. Then when you come to England you will be fluent like me,' she insisted.

'Okey dokey!'

'Proper English, not this shit slang language,' she ordered.

'Okay, how are you today?' Vasile quickly recovered.

'I'm great. It's quiet today; just two old ladies chatting old lady talk.' Then herself bored of typing, she slipped out into the passageway to call Vasile.

'For a minute,' she spoke. 'I thought they were going to surprise me because one of them wanted to talk about some new exciting app that had something to do with an oil company,' she laughed. 'But they must have lost interest or forgotten like old ladies do, because they didn't talk much about it at all.'

'What's the name of this app?' asked Vasile, with a keen curiosity.

'I will not tell you my love, because I know what you will do,' she said, and swiftly changed the subject.

As Anna continued to tell him about how she was missing him, Vasile opened Google on his phone and tapped in three words.

app oil company

Within a few seconds, numerous news articles appeared about an oil company called Sand Oil that had launched an app that facilitated free comprehensive car insurance, if customers perpetually filled up at their stations.

'Wow, that's a cool deal!' he thought. 'Maybe I should look at this app and see if I can cause disruption to this little venture. It could be worth thousands if I use my ransomware. Or maybe I could add another offer and give out free pet insurance,' he laughed, returning to WhatsApp.

'Yes, my darling. I will come to England very soon and we will look for somewhere to live and make a proper life together.' It was what Anna wanted, a normal life away from cybercrime - but first he would hack this oil app, sell the stolen data and demand huge sums of money to release them from ransom. This could be the big last job he'd been looking for.

'My darling, I have a surprise for you.'

Anna listened intently.

'I've bought a one-way ticket to London Heathrow. I figured it was time to give up this crazy game and lead a normal life.' His girlfriend was in tears. This was her dream come true.

They said their goodbyes and sent kisses on WhatsApp after ending the call. Going back to their separate lives, Anna went to serve another customer, while Vasile opened the app store on one of his phones, found the Sand Oil app and clicked install. After a few moments, it was ready to use. Vasile had several smart phones and a collection of SIM cards from different service providers around the world, including more than one from the UK.

Vasile plugged a USB into his smartphone that connected it to his laptop, then ran a simple scan against the Sand Oil app. Nothing of value or usefulness that might provide a way of hacking in was detected. Then he tried a more complex scan, looking for back doors and secretly hidden passwords. It wasn't uncommon for developers to place a private function in the app that would allow access to engineers. It made debugging problems easier.

'Nothing,' he sighed. 'Maybe I need to reverse the phone screen and try the last scan again?' It was an old trick he had discovered literally by accident after dropping a smartphone a few years ago.

He ran the scan again. 'Mi-a picat fata!' he exclaimed in victory, and there on the screen was a login with the user ID and password already filled. 'Fuckin' amateurs!' he smiled, shaking his head with incredulity.

'The Wolf has pounced!'

Chapter 25

When the morning session closed after the introduction of the EcoPodOffice™, lunch was served in the main conference room adjacent to the auditorium. Charlie and Mike decided to skip the free Korean food, electing instead to get some fresh air and a sandwich at a local deli'. Chewing away on something that resembled bread, with cartons of coffee in front of them, they took stock.

'Well, I wasn't expecting that!' they both spoke, coming to the same quick conclusion.
Between them, they had been expecting something, anything, else – not an office in a box!

Charlie spoke.

'After all that research and development, all he could come up with is work from home? That is a surprise. Even so, the EcoPodOffice™ is a good idea. If, as a cloud-connected office worker, you don't need to travel to work but still want to make it feel as if you are going to work, then the Office Eco *bloody* Pod makes sense. But what about all those living in apartments outside the city?' That question had gone unanswered.

'You make a good point my friend. But let's not forget that there is still the afternoon session to look forward to. There's bound to be another surprise if this morning's sitting is anything to go by. There's a much bigger picture here that we're not seeing yet. Working from home has been around for years. It's

very popular and practical, we both know that.'
They nodded in unison.

'What's that smell?' Charlie stopped to ask, sniffing the air as he picked up some intriguing aromas.

Mike beckoned a waiter to ask if he knew.

'So, that's why the city smells as it does?' he responded, feeling a sense of awe after making out what the waiter had said. The odd aroma was all around them, and it was strong enough to cling to their clothes.

'Look over there,' Mike pointed.

In the distance, high above the sky scrapers, a yellow hue blanketed the sky, partially obscuring the sun.

'That's air pollution. It's the same in London on busy days when there's no wind to push it away or cloud cover to hide it. But surely that's not the smell?'

Charlie beckoned the waiter again, this time getting a more detailed answer with the mention of trees, lavender, jasmine and several other difficult to pronounce botanical names.

The waiter pointed to the street below where they could see swathes of giant bamboo and spider plants, and what looked like another familiar house plant, Golden Pothos, but Charlie wasn't sure of the context. All he could see was greenery draping from overhanging balconies, and creepers that wound around lamp posts making the city look more like a jungle than an urban sprawl.

'That's all rather interesting,' Mike said. 'Not only is Yeong Ji-Won advocating working from home to help tackle pollution, but the city authorities would appear to have already acted by cultivating a large range of well-chosen plants to counter the effects of pollution. These plants are cleaning the air. I told you, there's a bigger picture here that we're not getting!'

They looked at each other and wondered what was coming next.

The lunch hour passed quickly, with both businessmen still absorbed by intrigue and interest in the enveloping city aroma as they returned to the auditorium. Their seats still felt warm from the morning, so they soon settled down for the next presentations.

'I have an idea,' said Mike.

Charlie looked at him.

'What kind of idea?'

'Never you mind. Let's see what happens this afternoon.'

At half-past one, Yeong Ji-Won reappeared on stage, again to excitable applause. He steadied himself at the front of the stage and was about to speak when a lone voice piped up in the auditorium.

'I have a question Mr. Yeong.' Charlie looked around to see Mike standing up.

Politely, Yeong Ji-Won asked for Mike's name and a little of his background before giving him the floor.

'Mr. Yeong, I mean no disrespect to you, our esteemed hosts, the city authorities or the people of this great city, but you mentioned in your opening speech *The Soul of the City.* Yeong nodded. 'Sir, can you help me to understand *The Smell of the City?*'

Charlie leaned back against his seat, readying himself for an expected backlash from everyone around him, including Yeong himself.

The speaker reflected for a moment before answering.

'Mr. Day you are very observant, and I thank you for asking this question so respectfully and for your courage in doing so. In my opening few words this morning, I named the *BIG 10* problems faced by cities today. You may remember Environmental Conservation being listed as one of those big problems. Just under three years ago when we started working on the Soul of the City vision, my team and I wanted to identify and implement some early, quick wins. We turned to Environmental Conservation as one area that we thought could provide some early benefits, benefits that would help in the longer term.

'Mr. Day, not all solutions to mankind's problems lie in man-made technology. We at Chihye Electronics have long believed in harnessing the innate biological components of trees and plants, often referred to as (and aptly named), Natural Technology, because if we did not, then we, and ultimately all of humanity, would fail. In those early days, a silent partnership was created between Chihye Electronics and the Seoul city authorities to help address city pollution by planting thousands of new trees and sweet-smelling, flowering plants. It has long been known that plants are an aide to reducing carbon dioxide in the atmosphere, but recent experiments show that it goes much further than that. A plant process called *phytoremediation* removes air-borne toxins by absorbing the poisons through their leaves and roots.

'While the impact of this action has so far been marginal, largely due to an increase in traffic over the same period, we are confident that, as we reduce traffic pollution, we will see an incremental improvement in air quality.'

Warm applause broke out, and Mike turned to look at Charlie with raised eyebrows and eased slowly back into his seat.

Yeong returned to his agenda.

> *Ladies and gentlemen, I have two further announcements I would like to make. To help combat air pollution and add to the work we have already undertaken to improve the environment, please let me introduce to you our most advanced and environmentally friendly vehicles for the twenty-first century traveller; the EcoPodCar™ and the EcoPodBike™.*

The stage floor opened once more, but this time there were two apertures, one either side of the EcoPodOffice™. The applause started again. Two gleaming white vehicles rose in a stately fashion from the depths of the stage, sparkling as the overhead stage lights caught them.

> *Firstly, the EcoPodCar™ is fully battery operated with a top speed of 65 kph. Carrying four people, it has a range of 1000 km on one charge, with a full recharge time of 4 hours. It has four seats and enough room to carry several shopping bags and two inflight carry-on bags. The compact dimensions make it one-third smaller than the average four-person car today. Three batteries run the entire length of the car and use a unique recharging system designed by Chihye Electronics. Ladies and gentlemen, at Chihye Electronics we believe that this car is the closest any vehicle has ever come to achieving perpetual motion, while emanating absolutely no carbon emissions.*

Excited by the impact this breakthrough could mean for the future, there was even more rapturous applause, with people across the auditorium standing to cheer. But Yeong continued, dropping the punch line.

> *These cars are available for anyone to hire for only USD 12 per day, inclusive of comprehensive car insurance. This currently translates at just under 800KPW if you prefer to pay using Wan,'* he raised his voice. *'And the people of this great city will no longer have to own a car to use one. Just register, pay and drive! And parking is free across the city. I envisage that within two years we will be*

introducing the first autonomous versions gradually switching every vehicle over in five years.

The audience loved it!

Yeong! Yeong! Yeong!

Came shouts that filled every inch of the auditorium. The cries attracted the attention of door security outside, who came to see what the alarm was.
Mike looked at Charlie. He was right, there was a much bigger picture. Yeong and his team were reinventing the means of transport across the whole city. Offices on demand, cars on demand and presumably cycling on demand too with the EcoPodBike™.
As the chanting of his name died down and people sat once more, Yeong let out a big sigh of relief. He looked up, thanking his lucky stars that the EcoPodOffice™ and the EcoPodCar™ had gone down so well.
'Well that's a relief. Thank you everyone. Thank you. Maybe I should stop there, while I'm ahead?'
Chanting started again. *Yeong! Yeong! Yeong!* so he continued by shouting almost at the top of his voice as the excitement grew.

The EcoPodBike™ is free to use, and it's comes in both electric and manual versions, with two, three or four wheeled versions - it's the new Ride and Park!

The place erupted!

Yeong had delivered solutions to solve the problems of Traffic Congestion, Air Pollution, Infrastructure Maintenance, Environmental Conservation, and to an extent, countering the effects of global warming but there were still the unanswered questions of Costly Public Transport, Overcrowding, Security Threats, Unemployment in Young People and Population Growth.

When the excitement had eventually subsided, Yeong took a sip from his glass of cold water before continuing.

As you will appreciate ladies and gentlemen, we had for good reason kept many of our announcements today as secrets, but I am also pleased to inform you that, having started to work with the City Authorities three years ago, our discussions are ongoing. I would now like to present to you the Mayor of this great city, Dr Ku Kang-Dae.

There was more applause as Dr Ku arrived on stage, clutching a small scroll in his hands. He shook Yeong's hand firmly and turned to face the awaiting room. Dr Ku unrolled the scroll and launched into his speech.

> *Ladies and gentlemen, esteemed guests and visitors from far and wide, welcome! Welcome to this great city of ours. We are delighted to have been working in partnership with Chihye Electronics this past three years, and we are even more delighted with the new announcements, so well made today. My congratulations, Mr. Yeong.*

There was a huge round of applause as Yeong Ji-Won stood to accept the recognition bestowed on him. Dr Ku continued.

> *Solving the BIG 10 is not something Chihye Electronics can do alone, although I dare say, if we gave them the city, they probably would solve all our problems.*

Around the auditorium heads nodded in agreement.

> *Today, in Public Transport, Overcrowding, Security, Unemployment in the Young, and indeed Population Growth, there are still challenges to overcome. Today we announce the first roll out of fifty productivity centres spread across the city, that we are calling EcoHubs. Each EcoHub will contain at least one hundred EcoPodOffice™ units meshed together to form a highly connected office network. In his ground-breaking speech earlier, Yeong left one critical point for me to*

announce, as mayor of this city. Every EcoPodOffice™, EcoPodCar™ and EcoPodBike™ will be connected to a city-wide super high-speed optical mesh network, capable of carrying millions of megabytes of data every second. To date, in our limited trials at a secret location outside the city, we have been discretely monitoring the movement of people, transport and many other things. The Mesh Network, which by the way, already sits high above us all, has provided insights we never dreamed were possible.

Yeong stepped in.

Apologies, we have not yet explained the term Mesh Network. Basically, it can best be described as a very large communications fishing net that spans the city. So far, it has allowed Chihye Electronics and the city authorities to detect any device with an open connection, such as an IP address, Bluetooth or Beacon, et cetera. In the city trials, we found no issues in detecting our EcoPod range. In fact, we managed to detect many other open devices as well, which included one-quarter of a million cell phones, some twenty-thousand smart TVs, more than a thousand smart kitchen appliances, and - somewhat unexpected by my team and I – forty-two, ahem, personal stimulation devices!

Sniggering and giggles rippled around the hall. 'Great punchline delivery there,' chortled Mike to Charlie.

'Every box has been ticked, what a guy!' Yeong elaborated to address a key issue.

> *To quickly reassure everyone about their personal privacy, this breach happened because of a minor computer bug, which has now been identified and eliminated. But to answer the curiosity coursing through the minds of the more innocent amongst us, why would a vibrator need to have wireless connectivity and an IP address? This task was not something I could respectfully delegate, so I did some research and found that the model detected has a high definition video camera attachment with wireless connectivity, and a further option for remote operation. The mind boggles.*

The audience laughed again, and taking advantage of the uproar, while a few tried to conceal their rapid note-taking, just for reference.

'Charlie, I like this guy; I like him very much indeed. We need to find a way to connect with him and somehow get him over to the UK, or even for us to come back here to explore how we might work together.' Mike was completely blown away by Yeong's entire vision, presentation, delivery and not least - his humour.

'I agree. He's a genius, and we like genius.'

Dr Ku returned to the microphone as the other half of this most effective double act.

Ladies and gentlemen, with so much data to collect and analyse in the coming years, and with the huge potential to exploit this data for the betterment of Seoul, and the other cities across South Korea, and eventually improving lives in cities across the world, I am announcing today, in partnership with Chihye Electronics, that, if they achieve the right grades in their important Suneung exams, we will be giving 60,000 young people in our city the opportunity to become data analysts, to help us solve these remaining problems so we can redefine the Soul of the City.

Yeong and Dr Ku shook hands vigorously, while deafening shouts and screaming rose up around them, from the auditorium and out to the doorways. The ovation continued for several minutes until finally, Mr. Yeong Ji-Won and Dr Ku Kang-Dae bowed for one final time and left the stage. They were exhausted, the audience was exhausted, as were Mike and Charlie. It had been a truly memorable day with so much to reflect upon.

'Truly amazing stuff, but I was a bit surprised they didn't mention having an app as well,' Charlie murmured.

'Bingo!' thought Mike. 'Houston, we have lift-off!' he winked at Charlie. 'Mate, we need to get an appointment with Yeong and Dr Ku, before we leave town tomorrow. We need to strike now.'

As Mike and Charlie continued their conversation, a young lady approached, bowed and handed them both business cards and elegant hand-written invitations.

'Looks like we've got our appointment at the closing drinks reception tonight,' Charlie said.

'You took the words right out of my mouth,' as Mike began to sing *Bat Out of Hell* and perform a little happy dance.

'Come on old man, let's get a beer and talk over what we've heard today,' Charlie said as he guided Mike to the main exit. It was getting dark outside. The S*mell of the City* was ever present. The air was cooler, thereby reducing its potency. The bright sunlight was turning to shadows and Seoul's volume had increased - rush hour was now in full flow. They imagined a future city full of hi-tech office pods, electric cars and bikes, and considerably less traffic on the roads.

'Maybe Yeong was right. Smart Cities can't just be about technology. They're more about Smart Management.' Mike concluded as they entered their hotel foyer, making a beeline for the bar.

Chapter 26

Following the young driver Chris Reid's death, the police retained all evidence from the scene of the accident including Chris' smartphone. This was passed to the police laboratory for examination, with the analysis being delivered the following day. PC Townsend contacted Sand Oil Insurance to make them aware of the situation.

A representative from the company looked at the data, especially the warning messages that had been sent and received, but never read. The log showed the following:

> *Registration completed at 14:05:02*
>
> *Code Entered and Acknowledged at 14:22:47*
>
> *Warning Message: You are travelling at 52 mph in a 30mph zone. Slow down!*
>
> *Time: 14:26:15*
>
> *Warning Message: You are travelling at 70 mph in a 50mph zone. Slow Down!*
>
> *Time: 14:57:25*
>
> *The fifth warning message was followed by a Red Alert.*
>
> *Red Alert: You are continuing to drive dangerously. Calm down and slow down!*
>
> *Time: 16:35:19*

> *Red Alert: Your continuing illegal driving behaviour is putting you at risk of losing your insurance cover. Calm your speed immediately, drive within the law and road conditions, or your insurance will be terminated.*

Then a final Red Alert arrived just after 5pm.

> *Red Alert: You have failed to comply with the Terms and Conditions of the Sand Oil Car Insurance policy – your cover has now been cancelled! Note: Your cover is cancelled.*

A Sand Oil Insurance representative called PC Townsend to explain the findings.

'According to our records, the young man in question had persistently ignored warning messages, continuing to drive at speeds beyond national speed limits. In total he was warned seven times before we had no choice but to cancel his insurance. Our records also show that he assented to the Terms and Conditions. Our app is designed to reject registration from anyone who has not read, or appears not to have read, the Terms and Conditions.'

'I see,' said the officer. 'Can you send me over all the information you have including a copy of the Terms and Conditions?'

'Sure. That's no problem. Just let me have your email address and it'll be with you in just a few moments.'

PC Townsend read his email address out loud and turned to face WPC McCarthy who had been listening intently.

'Chris Reid had been driving at excessive speeds pretty much all afternoon and didn't heed the warning messages or comply with local speed restrictions?' she repeated for confirmation.

'That's about it,' answered her colleague. 'At the time of his death his car insurance had been revoked. A small consolation but at least no one else was involved.'

'Not so small for his parents. When are you going to give them the findings?'

'After I've checked out this app for myself, read the records from Sand Oil Insurance and got an opinion from our technology lab. A young man has died so we must be certain of our findings before informing his family, and before submitting our report to the superintendent. After that, the coroner will then determine the Cause of Death, and sadly the parents will have to live with that information and their loss for the rest of their lives.'

'Such a waste of life, and so young,' said the WPC as she walked away shaking her head in sadness. 'Such a sad waste.'

After a few more calls to Sand Oil Insurance and the report from the Police Technology Lab, PC Townsend added his final statement to the report and submitted it to the superintendent for review and the onward journey to the Coroner. The file was slim; small recompense for the life of a young man.

Two weeks later, the coroner passed a verdict of death by dangerous driving. As he gave the decision, he looked at looked at Mr. and Mrs. Reid who were present at the proceedings – '*case closed*'.

After the coroner was leaving the hearing room, he saw Mr. and Mrs Reid in the corridor.

'I am very sorry for your loss. There are no words I can say that will be of any comfort to you. Your son didn't take the responsibility of driving seriously enough, and consequently it cost him his life. Please accept my condolences.'

WPC McCarthy led Chris' distressed parents out of the building for a final few words. They always knew their son had been driving dangerously that day. They were sadly aware of all the warning messages issued to him via the app, and the fact that at the time of his death his car insurance had been revoked.

The policewoman took them to one side, speaking softly, she said 'We've been in touch with the insurance company. They too are saddened by what happened, and while they accept no liability for what happened, they would like to make a good will gesture towards all the costs you have incurred following the accident and any other related costs you are likely to incur over the next 12 months. They emphasise that such good will in no way makes up for the loss of your son. They accept that the app was new and perhaps Chris needed to spend a bit more time familiarising himself with the Terms and Conditions before driving. That said, even if he had read them all, he might still have ignored them. Sand Oil Insurance would like to offer you £50,000 but they wanted you to confirm acceptance before you received a cheque unannounced in the post. I hope this hasn't upset you too much. Can I say yes on your behalf?'

The bereaved parents looked at each other, both with eyes reddened, and faces drawn with grief. With tears and mixed emotions, they both agreed. WPC Townsend expressed her sorrow one more time then later, called Sand Oil Insurance with the confirmation. Three days later, the cheque arrived in the post, along with a sympathy card.

Chapter 27

Mike ordered two cold beers at the bar. It was early evening. The hotel bar was mostly empty, and Mike and Charlie sat in a corner quietly chatting.

'A toast to the brilliance of Yeong Ji-Won.' Both men raised their glasses and swiftly emptied them, relishing the refreshment. 'Two more bartender please,' Mike indicated across the bar top.

'Okay Mike, spill the beans, what did you think of today?' Charlie asked with impatience.

'Bottomline, we've been disrupted - or should I say Sand Oil and Gas has.'

'What do you mean?' asked his confused companion.

'Electric cars mean no fuel, at least not of the type provided by Sand Oil. And the Pay and Drive scheme, means a lot of people will have no need to own a car or have their own comprehensive car insurance. Remember what Yeong said, *Only 12 USD per day, inclusive of comprehensive car insurance and free parking.*

'Shit! Shit! Shit! When do we tell Sand Oil?'

'We don't!' said Mike. 'Yeong's disruption won't have any impact outside South Korea for a few years, and by that time Sand Oil will have moved on to Phases 2 and 3.'

'You didn't mention a Phase 2 or Phase 3? I'm hoping that me and Jo will be able to take a nice holiday together in a few weeks. I've not planned for any Phase 2 or Phase 3.'

'That reminds me (and it's been puzzling me), what does your Jo do for a living and did you find out any more about that student kid? The one who designed all the app security?'

'Ah! I'm glad you asked me about him.'

A couple of drinks in, and Charlie had a bit of Dutch courage and decided now was the time to come clean.

'It's like this Mike, Adam, the student, is Jo's son, or so she's says.'

'Go on!'

'Jo explained that he was very good at information security, especially websites and apps, and since we badly needed someone to secure the app, I thought it was a good idea to give him a go. To our advantage, he turned out to be more than very good.'

'And Jo, what does Jo do?'

'Ah! That's a tad more difficult to put my finger on, but she did let slip in conversation that she has something to do with the security services, or something.'

'Bloody hell Charlie, really? I knew there was something fishy about that kid.'

They both stared into their drinks, almost hypnotised for a moment or two, before Charlie broke the silence.

'He can't be just another bloody student. He can't be Jo's son either, it doesn't make sense. He's got this accent Mike, Eastern European, I'd say.'

'You've got to be kidding me! Jo's accent is South London. Didn't your alarm bells go off?' Mike quizzed.

'Well...'

Mike cut in again

'He's got to be a bloody plant? Why would she do that? What's going on? Did Jo put him there to exploit something to do with our app? That's got to be why she's been very coy about what she does – but then again, she wouldn't be allowed to talk about her work anyway, sworn to secrecy and all that, but even so...' his words trailed off, hoping for his friend's sake that his and Jo's relationship had true substance, despite what was unfolding.

'I'm beginning to understand why the kid went to such great lengths to create an such elaborate game in our app. It's great security but they're definitely up to something and we need to find out what,' Mike affirmed.

'Good job you didn't tell me earlier Charlie, as I would never have agreed to any of it. All we can do now is hope that if any ship's going down, we're not on it.'

Two more beers arrived on their table. Charlie tried to change the subject.

'And what's this about two extra phases?'

'Sorry, I'm not at liberty to say. I'm sworn to secrecy.' They laughed. The beer was taking effect.

'But coming back to our app for a moment, I'm sure there must be a way to link it with Chihye Electronics' Eco range. There's a perfect link in that we are focusing on the driver whilst they are all about people working, driving, cycling and walking. But that's not where I'm going with my thinking, although that's probably where we need to start to build trust and credibility. No, my thinking is much broader.'

'I hate it when you talk in riddles. Spit it out man.'

'Okay, my university lecturer buddy,' as Mike prepared to raise his voice. 'Logistics! The Internet of Things, global security, Big Brother!'

'Eh! What? I don't understand,' as Charlie showed his puzzled face.

'Okay I'll explain. Chihye Electronics now has the basics for the development of a sophisticated tracking system. With access to such a phenomenal amount of collected data, they will soon need to employ thousands of bright young kids to help them make sense of it. When you strip all this back to basics, it's effectively about tracking moving objects that can probably lead to real-time decision making, automated learning, problem self-diagnosis and auto-resolution. What if this same vision was applied in different circumstances, such as logistics? The data collection, preparation and machine learning algorithms alone are worth a fortune. Get my drift?'

'Errrrrr no!'

'For fuck's sake Charlie, you're the intelligent one. Can't you work it out?'

'Not until after another beer,' he said, signalling the bartender for two more.

'I'll give you a very basic example, and hopefully your tiny brain will work it out. Take the High Street.'

Charlie butted in, 'What High Street?'

'I don't know, any High funckin' Street!' They both giggled like kids.

'Is that the High Street in Funckin or the Funckin High Street?' causing both to laugh some more. It was the first time in weeks they'd had a drink, and it showed. They laughed and giggled, enjoying the release.

'Bartender, two more beers please - and make it snappy!'

Charlie was on the wrong side of protocol.

'Sorry bartender I didn't mean that.' He lowered his voice.

'Make it funckin' snappy.' They both exploded simultaneously, so loud it was heard in the reception area. Within seconds, the hotel manager approached.

'Gentlemen, I am very happy to see that you are having a great time in our hotel. It gives me great pleasure to see our guests enjoying themselves, but gentlemen I have to ask you to respect the enjoyment of our other guests.'

Charlie couldn't look Mike in the face for fear he would make things worse.

'Come on my friend, let's go out and leave these people in peace.'

They finished their beers, signed for the bill and walked out, onto the street.

'Now what?'

'Taxi!' Mike yelled.
'So, that's what!' affirmed Charlie.
A taxi pulled up and they jumped in, wrestled with the seat belts and finally clicked in. The driver was quite young, with dark hair gelled back behind his ears. Mike drew his head back, opened his eyes wide and tried to refocus.

'Mister Taxi Driver we, as in me and my friend here, want to go to a very nice bar where we can drink beer and eat nice food.'

'Okay, okay,' acknowledged the driver, 'If you are looking for company from girls, I can take you to a very good Whiskey *talk* Bar. Or if you want a few girlfriend snuggles and some little extras, I know where the best Kiss Room is. But no 2 cha for you there. If you want 2 cha, I know verrry gooood places.'

'Shit mate! 2cha? Cha-cha-cha? We don't want to go dancing? No mate, just beer and food. We'll leave the girls and the cha-cha-cha to you, okay?' Charlie hoped he was clear.

'Okay! I know a verrry good place with good 2cha-cha-cha, so if you change mind, go next door.'

'Ha-ha, the old boy's even got a sense of humour,' roared Mike.

'I think *2 cha* means sex, not dancing,' whispered Charlie.

The taxi drew up at a bar called Sexy Tony's. Next door was also called Sexy Tony's.

'We've landed on our feet Mike, me old mucker, landed on our feet.'

Mike was checking out the street whilst Charlie had entered the bar and sat down at the first free table he could find. Seconds after ordering, two bottles of Hite appeared, as if by automation.

'Hello sir, your beers. If I may help in any way, please do not hesitate to ask. My name is Sarah and I am your host for the evening.' Her English was perfect, as was everything else about her.

Mike arrived, looked at his drink and sat down.

'Where the funckin' are we?'

Charlie started to sing.

'Somewhere over the rainbow, beers in hand….' but that was all he could remember of that version.

Mike steadied himself as he leaned around the table towards his good friend.

'Mate, we need to ease off this shit. I can't exactly remember the last time I had a drink but I sure as hell know I've had one or two now. If we're gonna make this drinks reception tonight, we need to ease off and drink some coffee.'

'I agree,' Charlie replied, swaying back and forth without any argument, 'but before we do, can we have two, just two more, tiny beers? Now close your eyes and I'll tell you when to open them.'

Mike reluctantly closed his eyes for what felt like ages, but it was only a few seconds.

'My friend, I give you Sarah and a very popular Korean drinking game.'

'Oh fuck!' shouted Mike, with a laugh. 'No funckin' way. I will split my sides.' He scanned Sarah. 'Mind you, she's lovely.'

'Mr. Mike Day, I've never engaged you in one of our famous drinking games, and I don't expect you to drink it, given your humble background, but it would give me great happiness and satisfaction if you would accept this challenge?' Charlie was loving it! He knew Mike could not refuse but he was interested to know how he was going to wriggle out of the predicament.'

'Whoa! Whoa! Whoa! If I drink this beer on the table and what's inside that weird looking drinking thingy, then there's no way we're going to the party tonight. Not turning up would be a sign of disrespect.'

Drinks reception was now a *party,* such was the effect of the beer and he happy mood they both shared.

A curious audience was building around the bar and other hostess girls started to notice the two English guys' adventurous attitude and take more interest in them.

'We need to deal with business first Charlie, then we can party, okay?'

'Aww, but we're having big fun, and the ladies are soooo…. And all I know is,' his friend replied, with a small burp in between, 'you are drinking what's in that thingy, even if it takes you all funckin' night.'

'Okay, but I have an idea first. Do you trust me with my idea?'

'Ooh, we're going to a *Norebang* are we?' Charlie squealed. 'Are we, are we Mike, say we are!' feigning ridiculous excitement for his own amusement.

'No, you fool! I'm talking about the party, the drinks reception tonight. I say we send a gift with our profound apologies and invite Mr. Yeong and Dr Ku over to the UK as our guests, all expenses paid. What do you think?'

'You're a genius Mike. Now get that funckin' drink down your neck before you get a penalty!' laughed Charlie, much too drunk now to be of any use to anyone.

Mike whispered in Sarah's ear. He gave her the invitation card carrying the address of the reception and trustingly, handed over USD $250 from his wallet and some extra for her effort.

'Sarah,' he said seriously, 'I would like you to arrange delivery of this very important gift. It must reach the recipient tonight, and you must follow my exact instructions. Okay, my instructions might feel a little weird, but I assure you this is not disrespectful, so please follow them exactly.'

Nodding, Sarah disappeared into a back room for a few moments. When she reappeared, Mike was beckoned to approve the details.

'Perfect!' Mike smiled reassured. 'Perfect.'

'Sir, I will take care of this. It will be delivered exactly as you have stipulated.' She was certainly captivating, and as Charlie had noted, spoke *with perfect English.*

'Sarah, one more thing. How do I complete this challenge without actually drinking all of it?

'That's easy. You invite me to share it with you. No man can doubt your integrity for such reasoning and your friend will enjoy it even more.'

'Oh, wow thank you! I owe you,' he said, succumbing to the pleasure of being professionally beguiled.

'For sure, I may take up this debt one day. I have never been to London and would like to meet the Queen. Is it possible?'

'After today, anything is possible in my world.' He handed her his business card.

Mike returned to the party. Charlie was surrounded by three girls who were helping to get him more and more into the party spirit.

'My friend, I accept your challenge. And I would like to honour you in return by inviting our host Sarah to share the experience.'

Charlie clapped loudly and egged them both on. The bar was full, and everyone's eyes turned to Mike and Sarah.

Sarah whispered, 'Just remember what I told you.'

The music played loud as they both raised the strange vessel and began to drink. Mike stopped after a few seconds for dramatic effect.

'You just said *drink it,* you didn't say drink it all in one go.'

Sarah was finished before Mike, but Charlie didn't care; he was enjoying the show.

The shouts from the bar crowd increased the more Mike drank.

'Gunbae! Gunbae! Gunbae!'

He completed the challenge and was warmly embraced by his friend. It was Charlie's turn now, only he didn't have a secret weapon like Sarah. At just after one in the morning, they left the bar. Mike had eased off the booze after the drinking challenge and was supervising Charlie into the taxi and a little later did the same to ease him out of the taxi into the hotel. Charlie was a wreck and Mike didn't feel much better.

While they were still at Sexy Tony's a few hours earlier, as planned, a gift was delivered to Mr. Yeong Ji-Won at the Chihye Electronics drinks reception. Yeong pulled the accompanying card from the package and cut it open. It read,
'Dear Mr., Yeong, with deep regret we are unable to join you in your triumph and celebration at tonight's reception. The *Soul of the City* vision is ground-breaking. You and your team of experts are a credit to your city and country. We hope that much good fortune and happiness reaches your door. It would be our great honour to meet with you again. Until we do, we hope our small gift is received in the well-meaning humour with which it is intended.'

It was signed; *Our very best wishes and apologies, Mike Day and Charlie Duke, 3D, London.*

Yeong remembered Mike Day and his question in the auditorium about the *Smell of the City*. He had taken Mike's business card and tucked it inside his pocket. He nodded.

'Fine words,' he thought. 'I will meet with these people again.'

With curiosity, he started to unwrap the gift. Tearing the paper with vigour he caught some writing on the side of the box. It read, *The Pleasure Seeker: The ultimate in sensual pleasure*. It was one of the models detected in city trials.

This was the last thing he had expected, but he laughed loud and long at the friendly, silly gesture.

Chapter 28

After an extended period of disruption for so many people, Mike and Charlie got back to work, following their uneventful but rather hungover return journey from South Korea. Mike made his usually weekly call to update Frank Delaney, and Charlie did the same with the Sand Oil Operations Director. Everything was still going better than expected. Frank Delaney was giving brief updates to his Board but nothing formal would be presented until the quarter end, which was fast approaching. He would also have to update the City of London Stock Exchange.

In Dorchester, Gloria Stenson had been busy researching new ideas for her business and had several times sought out Beth over lunch for inspiration. Her brother-in-law Andrew Dodd had since made his peace with his wife Kate and had made a special solo trip to Gloria where he took her out to lunch and apologised. Gloria quizzed him on the practicalities of the Sand Oil App and used the information in her research.

Meanwhile, the Romanian couple, Anna Sala and Vasile Lupei, continued their distant relationship, whilst Anna pursued new avenues, continuing to make enquiries about Marku, her missing brother. With Vasile now congratulating himself on the certainty that he had hacked the Sand Oil app, he looked forward to publishing the stolen data on the dark web to claim a successful hack and to further increase his fame and notoriety.

Despite his possible misgivings, Charlie continued to see Jo, although he tried to be a little more alert than before. He now held Jo under a greater level of suspicion, rarely mentioning the Sand Oil app. They just did normal things like normal people and left their work where it belonged, in the work place. Adam had presumably disappeared back into university life, but occasionally, he would drop into the 3D office to see how things were going.

John Calcott had been frantically trying to save his company and had called all his industry peers and directors together to urgently look at options. At some point, just like Frank Delaney, he would need to update The Stock Exchange. In desperation, Calcott had called in a favour at the Competition and Markets Authority, claiming that what Sand Oil was doing was illegal and that it should be stopped immediately.

Business expert Peter Langley had stayed in touch with Mike and Charlie to provide a helping hand in interpreting some of the insurance related data they were seeing about the disruption. It was proving to be a very useful partnership.

On the other side of the world, Yeong Ji-Won continued to work with the Seoul City authorities on the rollout of the *Soul of the City* vision. There had already been a lot of interest from outside South Korea and Yeong would spend more and more of his time travelling around the world presenting his vision. It was not long before he would visit the UK as Mike and Charlie's guest, and they would explore how they might work together. Dr Ku, the mayor of Seoul, was so busy with the rollout that he couldn't spare the time to travel.

And the arrogant, Lenny Tall continued to breach the contract he'd agreed with 3D.

Chapter 29

After drawing conclusions about Jo and her so-called son Adam, Mike asked that he, Charlie and the lad meet at the 3D offices, to go through the app security in more detail.

'We have a hacker in Room 1. Not sure if it's a he or she but let's call it a *he* for now,' explained Adam.

'He thinks he's stolen personal customer data and will most probably put it up for sale on the dark web, as well as announcing his personal success at hacking the app.'

Adam continued.

'Room 1 is best described as a corner turret of a four-turret castle. Our visitor has a challenge to complete before he is seemingly (by what he's thinks is his own skill), allowed to progress inside the outer castle wall to the next turret, or Room 2.'

'So, how does he get out of Room 1?' asked Charlie.

'It's quite simple really, but you'll only know how to do it if you're an experienced hacker. Basically, Room 1 looks just like the app code with a bit of personal data lying around. All he needs to do now is scan the code and find out if there's a back door.'

'And what is this back door?' asked Mike and Charlie in unison.

'We'll, I've hard-coded encryption keys into the software. He won't be surprised to see them because he'll assume, we were so busy trying to get the app out on time, that we took a short cut on encryption. As far as he is concerned, we are amateurs and it's important that we maintain that perception in his mind. Why? Because he will then take on the mindset of an amateur to figure out what to do next i.e. How to get from Room 1 to Room 4.'

'What happens when he gets to Room 4?' Mike was keen to know the final part of the elaborate game.

'Shit happens. We'll have him exactly where we want him, although he won't know it until it's too late. Then we'll turn up the heat and land him in deep shit.'

'What if he decides he doesn't want to play? Surely, he'll find a way out before we can reach him?' Charlie asked, with heightened curiosity.

'Yes of course he'll find a way out, but he can only leave if we let him. Rooms 1 and 2 are about the way in, whereas Rooms 3 and 4 are about the way out. Once he lands in Room 4 (and he will, because hackers tend not to give up), he'll think he's fully hacked into the app, stolen an abundance of customer data, stolen admin user credentials and found a way to generate eight-character codes that will allow him to get free car insurance for all his mates and anyone else who wants to get a freebie, without buying petrol from Sand Oil. Hell, he'll probably even find a way of selling them on mega cheap to make some extra money'

'Do I actually want to know what happens when he or his mates try to use these codes?' Mike asked feeling unsure.

'Yes, you do - but if I told you both now, it might spoil the surprise later. Don't worry, it's just a bit of fun and should appeal to your sense of humour, as well as the hackers! Adam had his fingers crossed. He had no clue what the surprise was later nor did he know anything about the hacker. It was just his own embellishment to a storyline that had gone way beyond Jo Daley's brief.

'What about his circle of friends?' added Mike.

'They won't find it quite so funny - well at least some of them won't. It just depends on how well or badly he's connected – if you know what I mean?'

'Okay, let's pick up this conversation up another time.' Mike requested.

Mike was intrigued to know what was meant by *it depends,* and shifted his eyes from Adam to Charlie, shooting him an emphatic glance which summoned Charlie to join him outside.

'I think this conversation has just confirmed my suspicions. He's got to be working for New Scotland Yard and his boss is probably Jo. What's Jo's last name?'

'Daley, Jo Daley', uttered Charlie, now beginning to feel that he had been used.

'Here's what we'll do. My guess is, that at some point soon, Adam will leave us for good. It will probably be after some fake urgent call from home. Just keep an eye on him and when he does decide to leave, don't make a big scene. Just say how sorry you are to see him go and wish him well. But for fuck sake, don't ask him to reconsider and stay!'

The two men nodded in silent affirmation.

'In the meantime, I need to call Frank Delaney and make him aware of the "fake hack", and what he should do if it reaches the media.'

Chapter 30

Three months into the disruption, Mike and Charlie were pawing over the latest data. The app had been designed to harvest information about users such as their behaviour behind the wheel, and a little about their spending patterns. Useful correlations between the data was still limited. Charlie was still working on the big data models.

'Let's start with the more obvious facts, then go a little deeper,' Mike suggested knowing all too well that they both wanted to delve deeper immediately and ignore the top-level numbers.

'Let's start with registrations, age profiles, driving behaviours and then let's look at whatever correlations we do have.'

Charlie used the data graphics tool on his tablet to pull up a basic snapshot. Gone were paper reports and static data points. The guys had created a flexible, small data model, and by using a highly flexible software tool, they could instantly cut the data into however it was required.

Charlie started to talk through the details,

> As of the end of 2017, there were estimated to be 33m cars on the road in the UK.

> In the 3 months since the app was launched, 12 million drivers had registered on the app, approximately 36%

> *The demographic between the age groups was skewed towards the younger generation with 74% of all drivers being under the age of 25.*

> *The geographic spread was universal cross the country, except in those locations not covered by Sand Oil filling stations.*

'Charlie, it would be interesting to know if anyone has managed to register from these locations? It would be interesting to assess if there could be a case for Sand Oil extending their reach. And I'd also like to know if any driver leaves their base location to travel specifically to fill up at a Sand Oil station.' They continued to explore the data.

'We already have more young people using the app than forecast. It means that the lifetime value of those drivers has increased, so we need to revise some of our model forecasts. What does the app survey tell us?'

> *Ninety-nine percent satisfaction across all the demographics.*

'Any ideas why it's not one hundred percent?'
'Yep! Queuing time at the Sand Oil filling stations in the early days. People chose to give this type of feedback using the app.'
'Great! And what's the average spend?' Mike asked with his typical curiosity.

'Quite a bit higher than the numbers Sand Oil provided. Remember, they only gave us the average purchase price of petrol but no age correlation. The average spend on petrol was £34.50 for the under 25s. We're seeing a figure of £46.10 which suggests when an under 25 visits a Sand Oil service station they are taking the opportunity to fill up their tanks to ensure they keep their insurance longer. It would be great to know for sure if the money they are saving on car insurance is being spent on more petrol. And ever better, if we could find out what additional non-petrol goods are being purchased. Pity our model doesn't extend to the final purchase value at the till, let alone the cubic capacity of the engines being supplied so we can gauge an average of miles driven per tank. We've got petrol-only purchase data which is not good enough for our purposes. We need a break down of the full purchase amount, but overall, these numbers are pretty impressive!' Charlie concluded.

'Charlie, have a talk with Sand Oil Central Operations and ask when we are likely to start getting the enriched data we requested. They should be delivering it every day at this point. And I'll put a call into Frank Delaney as well.'

They moved on to review the driving behaviour data.

'Can we look at average journey distance, times, speeds and geographical spread, and can we correlate it with the traffic data of the same period? Did you add the simple predictive modelling with the customer rule sets and notifications we talked about?' Mike added.

Charlie tapped on the screen in three places, and new graphs and trends appeared on the screen. Charlie summarised.

'Average distance nine miles, average journey time 35 minutes, and geographically as you would expect, most travel in and out of cities during typical rush hour times of 07:00 to 09:30, Monday to Friday, with a massive switch to local travel on Saturdays and Sundays. It looks like the data model and the findings are representative of what we see from our own experiences, every day.'

'Okay,' Mike paused. 'Let's simulate what happens with the time of travel varied by a few minutes. Take the list of customers who typically set off at 07:00. Simulate starting their journeys fifteen-minutes earlier and link the results to average speed and average journey time.'

Charlie opened a small window on his tablet, selected the required data fields and entered the simulation conditions. After a bit more screen tapping, he waited for the model to recalibrate and deliver the results.

'Well Mike, that's very interesting. Those slight tweaks to the journey start times have reduced the average journey time to twenty-minutes.'

'Let's work out the average cost saving per journey and the potential reduced carbon emissions, allowing for fifty-percent of cars to have idle switches. Let's see what other golden nuggets you can dig out. I'm updating Sand Oil later today. Can you give me a summary of everything we have talked about, and grant me access to the data tool in case I need to use it later? I want to blow their socks off and ask for permission to deploy the customer notifications, so we can see if the simulation of *Hints and Tips* can become a reality this month.'

'Sure thing Mike, no problem. I've already dumped everything into a PDF so you can hand it out or send it as well, plus you've been set up on the data tool since yesterday. Just check your email again for the login details.'

Reassuringly, Charlie was one step ahead again. He was a brilliant technologist as well as a superb statistician. The small data was good, but they needed bigger data and more correlations to really exploit the potential of the Sand Oil app.

'And what's been happening on the dark side? Any more insights?' Mike asked, knowing all too well from his conversations with Adam that any widely reported or high-profile app would get the hackers excited.

Charlie tapped on the right-hand black box and immediately called up a list of hacking attempts.

'So far, we've traced a few hundred scans emanating mostly from Russia, China and Romania, and several from the CIA. I know this because I got Adam to place traces on any scans. And, wait for it,' he broke off. 'The Black Hat we talked about is, as of ten-minutes ago, actually in Room 4! He's published his hack on the dark web and is asking for $2m to expose his method and includes the details of a sub-set of our twelve million customers.'

'Okay, I'll alert Frank. I've already explained what he needs to do, and after this next phone call, he'll get on and do it.'

The call into Frank Delaney was swift and to the point. Their colleague acknowledged, and immediately informed his Director of Public Relations.

Later that day, Mike delivered the progress report to Sand Oil and was not surprised to be given the go-ahead for the customer notifications service.

As a sample test of over 50,000 push notifications were sent out the following day:

> *We've calculated that if you start your normal journey tomorrow ten minutes earlier then traffic is usually lighter and will save you time and fuel.*
>
> *Yesterday you're driving was great! Remember speed kills! Stay within limits!*
>
> *Alternative route: Go via King's Road and Chelsea to save time!*
>
> *Yesterday it was calculated that the average cost per mile was13.6p*
>
> *One warning message was issued yesterday! Try to make it zero today!*

Feedback and reports on social media suggested the messages had been welcomed by many of the drivers. Charlie sent a short email to Sand Oil Customer Operations who were monitoring the main social sites, and he didn't have to wait long for a response.

'Social media engagement is up almost 500% this evening. All very positive. Some people are reporting it was their least stressful trip to work in months. Others are telling us how much they enjoyed their commute for a change. One popular question; Any advice for the journey home?'

Mike smiled. It was a question he and Charlie had debated time and time again, but the data wasn't yet complete so he would have to let them know. In reply he wrote,

'Thanks for feedback. Very encouraging. Could you post this message please?

Re Journey Home: we are working on it and will advise once we have enough data points to be useful. Will notify each customer individually.

Mike and Charlie knew it was a more complex problem to solve. In the morning most people were traveling towards a common city destination. At the end of the day, they were of course, going in many different directions. In big data terms, a much harder problem to analyse and solve.

'The data will reveal more and more,' Mike thought. 'Be patient. Now, there is more than enough small data to digest.'

Chapter 31

Jo Daley was alerted by immigration that Vasile Lupei had entered the country. She had been aware of the Romanian ever since she joined the anti-cybercrime squad. In fact, he had been her first watch assignment. She called the Duty Officer at Heathrow.

'This is Jo Daley, New Scotland Yard. Tell me about your little find.'

'Yep, the subject in question is here,' said the Duty Officer. We found him after a spot check but allowed him to proceed as per instructions. Was heading off to Dorchester to meet his girlfriend, or so he said; his English was not so good.'

'Thanks. We know where he's going. We're tracking him now via his smartphone.' She hung up. Jo already knew that Vasile had planned to hire a car and drive south to Dorset.

She Googled 3D Mike Day and noted the office number from the results displayed. She would call him a little later for a chat. On the screen to her side, she followed the GPS blue dot as it travelled across the map, indicating exactly where Vasile Lupei was at any one time. The Wolf had now strayed into her patch and she needed to apprehend him at just the right moment. But first she needed to set some wheels in motion.'

Jo suddenly remembered a field operative surveillance report indicating that Anna, Vasile's girlfriend, often favoured a local café. She scribbled some notes and asked one of the nearby officers to dig out the document and make some discreet enquiries. Less than half an hour later, she reported back.

'Good, it looks like Anna might take her Wolf there for coffee sometime. A quiet café by the sea is perfect place for an arrest. All we have to do now is stake out the place and turn up when the time is right.'

She ordered the café be put under surveillance, and for a unit to be dispatched to instruct the manager to discretely ask his staff to take a short break when her team needed to commandeer the whole site for the specific purpose.

Looking at the operations room clock, Jo Daley decided it was time to contact 3D. She picked up her desk handset, flicked the voice muffler switch and called, asking to speak with Mike Day. It was time for her to reveal just enough for them to play along.

Mike was reading some of the latest comments on Facebook and Twitter when the re-routed call from reception reached his phone. It wasn't one of the many contacts in his address book, so he hesitated for a moment before answering, having decided it was a journalist looking for some information.

'Mike Day' he answered, in his assertive professional voice.

'Hello Mr. Day. I'm the officer in charge at the Cybercrime Unit at New Scotland Yard.'

Mike paused, gesturing to Charlie to come over, before he replied.

'OK Officer, you have my attention. What can I do for you?' He put the phone on speaker.

'How's my boy doing?'

'I don't follow your drift,' Mike played along. He was expecting a call but wasn't sure when.

'Ah, that boy - the student!' Mike looked directly at Charlie.

'Don't panic Mr. Day. We're not after your app or dismantling your little disruption. Our objective is somewhat different. It's just that we've piggy-backed on your app to get us close to our target.'

'Care to share the secret? I won't tell anyone - honest!' he said, making a childish face across his desk to the listening Charlie.

'That's classified Mr. Day, but I will share with you one thing; play along with our little game and everything will be OK. I'm only interested in my target, I don't care how many people you put out of work or provide zero-cost insurance to. I'm only interested in one thing - my target. Adam has assured me that the target already believes they have hacked into your app, and stolen the algorithm generating the 8-digit codes issued by Sand Oil. I'm also informed that a list of customer details has been extracted for sale on the dark web. Don't worry Mr. Day, what our target thinks is genuine, I can assure you is not. As soon as they publish any of the stolen data, they are going to get a big surprise.'

'Sounds great! Is there anything else I should know?'

The question hung in the air for a few seconds.

'By the way Charlie says *hello*.'

The line went dead. Jo Daley had a terrible sinking feeling. Everything was now out in the open and Charlie knew she had used him.

Chapter 32

After his call to the Competition and Markets Authority (CMA), John Calcott was anxious to hear the outcome. He had very few hopes left of stopping the Sand Oil disruption of his company and the wider industry.

After four weeks the investigation had been completed, and a report was produced in week five. The Lead Investigator called a press conference to announce the preliminary findings and to confirm whether a more comprehensive investigation would be required.

The press conference was attended by the usual business journalists. At the back sat Charlie and Mike. Trying to remain out of sight, they spotted John Calcott, lurking.

Right on time, the Lead Investigator stepped forward.

'Ladies and gentlemen. Today marks the end of an investigation into Sand Oil and its entry into the car insurance market through an innovative app that offers complementary comprehensive car insurance every time a registered user fills their car up with petrol.

'My team of investigators have carried out over 50 interviews across Sand Oil and 3D technology, as well as more than 200 interviews with members of the public, both users and non-users of the Sand Oil app. The initial findings have been collated, conclusions have been drawn and our recommendations are now being made.'

He paused for a moment adding to the tension in the room, then continued.

'It is the conclusion of the investigative team and me, as Lead Investigator, in this matter, that we can find no evidence of a breach of competition rules.

'Secondly, it is our finding that consumers are benefiting greatly from such an app and therefore conclude, that the product acts in the wider interests of the British public. Sand Oil and Gas, Sand Oil Insurance and 3D technology are henceforth free to continue their venture without restriction, and no further investigation is warranted at this time, if ever.'

There was a long shout of despair from John Calcott, followed by several crashing noises and angry outbursts. When the noise had died down the Lead Investigator completed the press conference.

'Finally, it is also concluded and recommended that such competition should be encouraged, even though it may result in job losses across the industry. Looking at the facts, it is the conclusion of the investigative team that, on balance the continued use of the Sand Oil app is in the wider interests of the British public and road safety. The competition is deemed fair, however disruptive to businesses dependent on, or the people within, the vehicle insurance industry.

'Thank you all. As usual, copies of the report are available on the table to my right or via download as a PDF from the website.'

Charlie looked at Mike. Mike stared back. They spoke in unison.

'Well that couldn't have gone any better.'

Chapter 33

At the start of the following day in the next instalment of his increasingly stressful week, John Calcott readied himself to meet analysts from the City. As CEO of Insurance Direct, he had not been looking forward to this at all. He envisaged there would be some tough questions that would be hard for him to dodge.

It had been well known in the market place for a while now, and was reflected in the share price drop, that Insurance Direct had been hit hard by the disruption, but *how hard?* was surely the question on the tips of the analysts' tongues.

Calcott shuffled uncomfortably in his tall back leather chair, awaiting the knock on the Board Room door. Once he had stopped shuffling, the notification came and in strode six City analysts, acting as though they owned the place, and who proceeded to take chairs, three either side of the table in a group as close to the CEO as possible.

Placed on the polished table before them were several copies of a slim document titled, "1H Update to the City." Without any prompting, the analysts picked up a copy each and began thumbing through the pages.

Calcott gave his usual, well-rehearsed introduction about the business and how it was performing in comparison with the same period, the previous year. While overall performance wasn't too bad, he then shifted to the outlook, based on the year-to-date but, especially based on the previous quarter. Performance had been dismal and was steadily getting worse as they moved from May into June and then into July. By the end of July, car insurance renewals were down ninety 99.7%. Of those who did renew, data revealed that a majority did so only because they didn't have a smartphone so couldn't access the Sand Oil app. Only a few others had renewed, seemingly untrusting of technology, preferring the old way of insuring their vehicles, despite the wide cost disparity.

In his twenty-five years in the insurance industry, Calcott had never seen the performance of a company drop off a cliff so dramatically. It was as though they had stopped trading, but the truth of the matter was precisely, with very few exceptions, that they had stopped selling car insurance. He continued.

'Ladies and gentlemen, the past three months have been the toughest in Insurance Direct's long and illustrious history. In all my years of experience, I have never witnessed anything like it. It's only a matter of time before this fall in sales will see us removed from the car insurance business completely. We have seen an unprecedented eighty-percent of our business evaporate in just over three months. Without renewals and new sales of general insurance, travel insurance and pet insurance, our destiny would see us going into administration in just over six months. The outlook is very bleak unless we can find a way to reverse the situation. At present, we don't have any robust options for solving the problem – unless we start giving away car insurance ourselves! Of course, we can't do that! After this meeting I will make a formal statement to the City.'

The outlook was bleaker than the City boys had expected. All had already started offloading shares, pensions units, bonds and anything else that gave them any sort of liability towards Insurance Direct. As far as they were concerned, Insurance Direct was close to *junk*!

'Mr. Calcott, will you step down as CEO, or do you plan to try to save the company?' asked Jay Patel, Chief Analyst, Redrock Consulting.

'To be honest Jay, I'd hadn't given it much thought. You'll appreciate that before Sand Oil entered the insurance business with their disruptive idea and technology, Insurance Direct was performing very well, and the outlook was good. The past three months have seen the rug pulled from underneath our feet in a spectacular way. Of course, we regularly consider our competitors' activities, and often adjust our pricing and strategy to ensure we maintain market position, but this is different. This is an oil company offering free car insurance! It's incredibly hard to compete on price when there isn't a price to compete with. I've had my Sales Directors, Marketing Directors and non-Executive Directors locked in rooms trying to find answers, but so far nothing hopeful has arisen. And yesterday, the CMA announced its findings after a four-week investigation and found in favour of Sand Oil.'

Jay Patel asked another, but this time obvious question, 'You have, of course, opened a dialogue with Sand Oil?'

'No, I haven't!'

Audible gasps were heard. Another analyst piped up.

'Forgive me sir, but given they have you by the short and curlies, don't you think it would be the least you should do? Maybe there's still something left of Insurance Direct that they might want, or that you could save?'

'It's a thought, I suppose. But do I really want to go cap in hand to the cocksuckers who are in the process of destroying 150 years of history, not to mention the potential of putting about 25,000 people out of work? And there's the wider insurance industry to consider too. This hasn't just impacted us; it's across the whole market. Every chief exec from Land's End to John O'Groats is wrestling with the same problem. Between us, we've had several conference calls and meetings since May and the impact is systemic across the whole industry. The only reason I'm giving you the heads up now, is because we are the largest, with thousands of shareholders, pensioners and pension funds trusting me and my team to deliver a good performance year on year.' Calcott stopped. He was getting emotional and needed to recompose himself.

'Thank you for coming, no more questions. I will update the City formally at 14:00 hours. You can get the rest of my update then. Thank you for your time. Please see yourselves out and I'd appreciate it if you keep this under wraps until five-past two. Have a better day than me.'

Calcott finally had a moment to compose himself and draw breath. He was aware that in only twenty-five minutes he would be making the defining speech of his career, or what was left of his it. It was a five-minute drive from his office to the London Stock Exchange. His chauffeur pulled up, careful to avoid trapping his passenger's door against the well-placed security bollards. Calcott was greeted at the entrance by an official who escorted him through the building. As he walked, the CEO felt like a condemned man about to face his executioner, with the penitential irony of having entered from Newgate Street not being lost on him. As he reached the first floor, he could see ahead of him the Forum Room, where he would soon be addressing the suits in rows of leather chairs, stretching to the back of the room. As he sighed from his soul, Calcott prepared to give the most important yet detrimental announcement of his entire career.
At two o'clock, and looking very shaky, he stepped to the podium, tapped the microphone then began to read his statement. The room was full of concerned looking journalists and other media types. It was eerily quiet for such a large group.

Mr. Chairman of the London Stock Exchange, ladies and gentlemen, over the next few minutes I will provide a trading update on Insurance Direct's recent performance. I will then take questions for a further ten minutes before giving a closing statement.'

Pausing momentarily for a sip of water, he straightened his back and lifted his head to scan the room. Every major news channel was represented. He could see the straight-faced long- standing reporters from the BBC, ITV, SKY and CNN, as well as two senior civil servants. Standing between them was Peter Langley, whom he recalled from the industry conference.

Mr. Chairman, ladies and gentlemen, until the close of April last, the performance of Insurance Direct continued in line with all expectations. Indeed, you will remember that following Q1, all our key indicators were reported as being good to strong. Since 1st May, we have witnessed a catastrophic change in performance.' Calcott then conveyed the same stark message he had delivered to City analysts.

Since 1st May, when Sand Oil launched its digital app offering free car insurance, there has been a stratospheric decline in the performance of our car insurance business, a decline Has extended across the whole industry. Car insurance renewals specifically, are down 99.7% with new customer recruitment registering an unprecedented drop of 99%. The income from our range of car insurance products is catastrophically low; so low that it is unsustainable.

Following the May launch, news of this unique and unprecedented disruption to the car insurance industry, spread like a huge wildfire, with sustained news bulletins from the TechWatch TV Studio heavily influencing opinion across all major social media channels. This downturn was so dramatic that if it were not for the breadth of our non-motoring range of insurance products, our business would be in ruins. That said, even our wider range of products will not keep our business model going for much longer, and therefore, as of today I am announcing a profits warning and substantial cost cutting exercise. With immediate effect, Insurance Direct is to cease new policy trading with all car insurance brokers, to instead concentrate its considerable efforts on what remains of our insurance portfolio. We will, of course, continue to honour existing car insurance policies as well as any customers who wish to renew with us to the end of the financial year. Car insurance is the bedrock for our other insurance products and without it, our business model fails.

Ladies and gentlemen, never in my thirty-five years in the insurance industry, has such an event rocked us to the core like this. My Executive Team and I have explored many options to defend our position in the market and we have also talked with our colleagues across the industry. We are all agreed; the outlook is bleak. We cannot compete on price when there is no price to compete with. We cannot compete on service when the service is fully digital, personal and continuously adding value, and we cannot bring our brand and legacy of trust to bear when social media and the market, rate the competition as "Exceptional".

We are on our knees. All we can do is get up, dust ourselves down and try to save as much of our proud and historic business as we can. However, there would seem to be one glimmer of hope. Only yesterday, after the Competition and Markets Authority made their announcement, I learned that there had been a hack of the Sand Oil app and a significant data breach had occurred. As an industry, we take our customer data security very seriously, but it appears Sand Oil doesn't give it the same priority!

The mention of a hack and data breach was his last desperate attempt to undermine and put to an end the rollout of the Sand Oil App.

Calcott stopped momentarily, took another sip of water from the glass on the podium. Looking up, he scanned the room again.

'I will now take questions.'

'John Willows, Goldman Financials. Are you expecting to announce further profits warnings?'

Calcott replied, 'I refer you to my previous statement regarding our outlook. Next?'

'Brian Dean, USA Today. Can you envisage such a disruption happening in the United States, or perhaps even globally?

'It's difficult for me to say as I don't have first-hand knowledge of those markets, neither do I know enough about the Sand Oil app or their plans. I will say though, that it would be wise for all markets to regard this disruption as a very serious threat. Using the core product from one industry against the core product of another, is not a situation we had envisaged. Nobody knows what will happen next, but it wouldn't surprise me if other industries started looking at their product range and began to consider the implications of something similar happening to them.'

The next journalist to ask a question was George McCaul of ITV News. 'Did you see this threat coming? Was it possible for you to take any steps to deal with it beforehand?'

'No, alas, we did not see it coming. Since then, we have looked under every stone, trying to find ways to defend our car insurance business against this type of threat. So far, we have failed to find any viable response. We just don't have the technology, neither do we have the buying power of Sand Oil.'

'Mike Day from 3D. Do you remember being warned about this a few months ago at the annual insurance industry conference? And was it not your view at the time, and I quote – *Do you really think people believe in all that digital scaremongering?*'

'Well sir, I really hope you believe in it now.'

'I'm not sure to what you refer, Mr..., whatever your name is. Final question! You, yes you over there. Your question please sir.'

It was exactly the kind of dismissive response Mike had expected. The barrage of questions came thick and fast.

'James Page, The Times Newspaper. What plans do you have for the 25,000 people who work for Insurance Direct today?'

'Our intention is to send a standard letter to all employees by close of business tomorrow; then begin a consultation process to discuss what steps need to be taken thereafter. Thank you for your time today.'

As Calcott uttered his final word, he'd already half turned towards the door. Wanting desperately to make a quick exit, he was instead swamped by reporters, all demanding answers to the questions they weren't given an opportunity to ask. The Stock Exchange's security shielded him from the barrage and the jostling that accompanied it. Finally, he was in the safety of a side room, a little shaken but glad he'd gotten through his ordeal and had taken a few questions. For a split second he felt much better until it dawned on him that from this moment, life would never be the same again.

His much-loved company lay in ruin, and he still needed to deal with much of the disruption's aftermath. It was the worst day of his now miserable life.

Chapter 34

The day after John Calcott made his statement, Frank Delaney was preparing to update the Sand Oil Board and then make his own statement to the City. He was excited and delighted with the latest results that Mike Day had shared with him.

The Board convened earlier than usual so that Frank could update the London Stock Exchange as soon as it opened. He reached the board room at seven o'clock, shook hands with the Chairman then turned to address the others present.

> *Mr. Chairman, members of the board, it is with great pleasure that I update you all on Sand Oil's latest performance and outlook to the end of this financial year. I will also take this opportunity to update you on progress that followed the deployment of our new app, and the timeline of events for the rest of the year.*

Frank's voice flowed like liquid gold.

> *First, may I start with headline statements of income and expenditure, and any exceptional items before providing the same for the Sand Oil app. May I also remind you of the sensitivity of what I am about to tell you. Officially our next quarterly statement is not due until the end of Oct for the period January to September this year but considering the*

> market disruption currently underway and the effect this is having on Sand Oil, as well as those being disrupted, it's important to keep you all informed of progress, then discuss and agree any change in strategy.

There was nodding and agreement around the room regarding the sensitivity of the statement. Frank turned on the vocal tap again.

> UK income is up ten percent, compared with last year, and is the largest quarterly increase on record. Costs remain relatively flat as expected, with no exceptional items. Mr. Chairman and members of the Board, this also represents the biggest annual increase in income ever recorded by Sand Oil. This has been achieved in three months, which is truly incredible. Not only are we selling substantially more fuel, but all our filling station outlets are reporting increased sales of other non-petrol goods such as coffee, sweets, magazines, and so on. The numbers are truly remarkable. We've had to increase our order levels with suppliers to keep up with demand.

This was the moment of truth. Was Frank's vision for a new era dawning for Sand Oil and Gas? He was a man on the edge of his seat, the excitement in his voice growing exponentially.

> *I would like to move on now to the Sand Oil app, and the disruption of the insurance market. The number of registered drivers now stands at well over 12m, increasing daily. Based on current numbers and spending patterns we are expecting to break through our income target for the year sometime in September. As you all know, that would represent a new record income for Sand Oil. I spoke with Mike Day earlier today to congratulate him and his team on progress. Mike reports no operational issues and everything is progressing as expected; in fact, better than expected, if I'm honest. He even assured me that the risk of cybercrime was minimal, although they were watching a development from Romania. I've been personally briefed on this matter and will deal with it in my statement to the City.*

Frank continued emptying his well of words.

> *I'm sure all of you have all been following with interest how the insurance industry is dealing with the disruption. If you look at the Top 10 car insurer's share prices before our app deployment compared with now, you will see massive falls. Yesterday, John Calcott, CEO of Insurance Direct made a statement to the City that included the words "The income from our range of car insurance products is*

> *catastrophically low; so low that it is unsustainable. We are on our knees!*

Frank paused for effect as board members gazed around the room in disbelief, aware that it was Sand Oil, and therefore they, who were destroying the car insurance industry.

The Chairman spoke.

'Frank, that's depressing news about Insurance Direct and the wider car insurance industry, but what are our new customers saying, and what's the wider perspective from the media and motorists?'

It was a good question, designed to put the focus back on what Sand Oil was doing for millions of consumers. Frank turned a page and began his answer.

> *Mr. Chairman and members of the Board, if the feedback from customers supplied by Mike Day is anything to go by, then consumers love it. In wider social media circles and through our own social media sites, it's clear that once people feel convinced that the app and the car insurance offer is legitimate, they are downloading and using it in droves.*

'And the media?' prompted the Chairman.

'Well, considering that most journalists are car drivers and therefore they too need car insurance, the feedback from the vast majority is extremely positive. One or two have mentioned the demise of the car insurance industry and the loss of jobs, but overall have taken a balanced view that the industry had been warned only a few months earlier, by Mike Day no less, but had ignored his warnings.'

'Frank! Is that it for now?' the Chairman checked.

'Just one further update, if I may, and this is something I'm sure the market and especially consumers will not be expecting. Just a few days ago 50,000 notifications were sent out to customers, advising them on how they could save time and money whilst driving. By making small adjustments to their driving routines, the early signs indicate that the data now available from the app can help our customers improve their journey times to work and reduce carbon emissions. Not only do they have the deal of the century, but we're saving them even more money, improving their quality of life and helping save the planet.'

Frank stopped again and waited for questions.

'Frank!' the Chairman called out.

'I want to learn more about what we're doing to the car insurance industry. Maybe we should be thinking about moving sooner than next year? Let's talk offline and decide if we need to convene the Board again. Maybe we will need to decide on Phase 2 sooner? If we leave it too late, it's possible there will be very little or nothing left.'

Frank agreed and pondered, while the Chairman shook hands with the departing members of the board.

'Maybe Phase 2 and Phase 3 should be brought forward?' He thought.

Frank Delaney delivered his statement to the City as expected, making special reference to the claim by John Calcott that the Sand Oil app had been hacked. He followed Mike's instructions, even though he wasn't sure he should, quoting that the Head of the Cyber-crime Unit at New Scotland Yard had personally confirmed the hack was a fake. If Jo could use Charlie, why shouldn't Mike use Jo? She was fair game.

Chapter 35

As she took her first morning coffee, Gloria Stenson was blissfully unaware that Frank Delaney had delivered a hugely upbeat statement to the Stock Market. Her world was a million miles away from the power-houses of big business in London, but decisions made in boardrooms could have positive as well as dire consequences for her business and the rest of the country.

Coffee finished, Gloria opened the shop door, before returning to her desk where she wrote,

'Offer a different insurance product but with a delightful twist,' smiling as she remembered her friend Beth's seemingly throwaway comment a few weeks ago.

'Something delightful and different?' She asked herself again and again.

Just as she pulled her chair in to start work, the door flung open to her surprise. She had no booked appointments and was a little taken aback.

In the three months since the disruption started, her business had been turned upside down. Previously loyal customers had deserted her and any new customers she might have hoped for, were extinct. Her visitor was Mrs Cartwright a customer of twenty-five years.

'Good afternoon Celia, please have a seat.' Gloria was her usual courteous self, even though she was distracted by her desire to continue her research into new product ideas.

'Good afternoon Gloria. Thank you, but I won't sit down because I've decided not to renew my car insurance.'

'Ah okay, Celia. Any particular reason why?' Gloria asked through courtesy rather than inquisitiveness. The Sand Oil app had destroyed her business and her ex-customers where saving hundreds of pounds at her expense.

'Well it's like this Gloria. The optician has said that my eyesight has deteriorated. Driving is now a little bit too dangerous. I've thought about it and decided to take the optician's advice, sell my car and use the bus instead. It's been such a difficult decision and you know how much I love my *Deirdre*.' Her eyes started to well-up.

'Come in Celia, take a seat and let's have a nice cup of tea together. You can tell me all about it.'

Reluctantly and a little sheepishly, Celia accepted the invitation. A huge weight had been lifted from her shoulders. She hadn't told anyone about her eyes, the optician's advice or the prospect of having to sell her little car, Deidre. It was a burden she had carried for a couple of weeks and Gloria, out of necessity, was the first to know.

Gloria made them tea and before long Celia had recovered her composure and was chatting away as if nothing had happened. Deirdre had been her only car, and like Celia herself, had become somewhat vintage. Deirdre was one of the family and the idea of parting with her was hard to bear.

Celia left the shop, a happier and more philosophical soul. Gloria reflected for a moment; 'At least I have my health. And thank goodness I don't have a Deirdre.' She laughed and set about her task of solving the problem caused by the Sand Oil app and the market disruption that ensued. Her business was down but not yet out!

After several weeks of research and mulling over many different options, she had worked out a way forward. She was ready to take the plunge. She ordered new business cards, two large posters and some leaflets. When they arrived three days later, she opened them with the excitement of a child unwrapping a birthday present.

'Gloria, now who's the genius!' she thought.

Before reading the text from the newly received poster out loud.

'Give yourself peace of mind – one insurance policy for all your household needs!'

She had removed all references to car insurance from her shop as well as from the signage above the main window in which she placed a new poster which now read:

General Insurance Broker

Gloria laid out her new leaflets, business cards and stepped outside for a moment to check the main poster was in the right place. It was.

All she had to do now was wait for her first customer. With no customers to speak of for a while, she was delighted when the shop door was eventually pushed open and in stepped Mrs Cartwright once more.

'Well hello Celia. How are you?' Gloria was very happy to see her.

'I'm very well thank you Gloria. I was just passing, and I saw in your window that you provide travel insurance. With my eyes being so bad these days and not able to drive Deidre, I've taken to travelling by bus, and guess what? I'm loving it. I never knew you could travel all over the country and even parts of Europe by bus. After a few trips around the United Kingdom, I've decided to go on a trip to Austria with my husband. He likes traveling around by bus too, but we don't have any travel insurance. Apart from insurance for Deidre, we've never needed any for travel outside of the UK before. And I thought, where on earth am, I going to get travel insurance? Just as those words had entered my head, I saw your poster so here I am.'

'Well, Celia you've certainly come to the right place. Travel insurance it is, and maybe I could interest you in one or two other things as well. You know me Celia, there's no hard sell; just a friend helping a friend.'

Gloria was back to her best, laying the ground like thick butter on toast. Celia would melt and Gloria would have her first new policy. She was back in business caring for those who preferred a more traditional pace of life with the personal touch in this increasingly faceless world. In a world turned upside down by digital disruption, Gloria Stenson was back. And *Deidre* was back too. Celia didn't part with her after all. She was one of the family just like Gloria.

Chapter 36

Scouring the hacked data, Vasile suddenly realised he had a done something crazy. He was shocked to find that the information wasn't genuine customer data at all. Starting at the top, he skimmed down row after row, hardly registering any of the names. As far as he was concerned, he'd hacked into the Sand Oil app database and had taken a copy of thousands of customer records. He had helped himself to all these records but was horrified to discover they could not be genuine names of real customers. Buried within the data were names like Blackeye, Terroriser, Lightwing, Z-bomb and The Finger; names that he and his former accomplice Marku, knew all too well. But there was one name listed that drained the colour from his cheeks - The Genie, a right-wing radical with criminal and terrorist connections who used the dark web to connect with underground gangs and international terrorist groups. The Genie was renowned for brokering deals against the system, any system, in any country, anywhere. Taking his name from the anti-hero in Aladdin's Lamp, rub him up the wrong way and this Genie would take murderous revenge.

Vasile stopped scrolling. If these most feared and secretive underworld operatives were to discover that he, Vasile Lupei, had a hand in their names and details being sprayed all over the net, his life would be in severe danger, and anyone else's who was close to him. 'Anna!' he cried out, instinctively.

As quickly as his frantic fingers could type, he removed the data file from sale, but it was too late. It had already been viewed, paid for in "doughnuts" and downloaded by several criminal gang members including, quite possibly, The Genie. It was only a matter of time before he would receive a message, a visit, or a phone call. It was only a matter of time before he would need to explain the situation to Anna and pursue refuge away from the web, mobile phones and anything else that could be used to track him or Anna down.

In her office, Jo Daley contemplated her next move. She had The Wolf in her sights and she too was ready to pounce. She picked up her mobile phone and made a call.

At the 3D office, Adam Barth was eating his lunch whilst checking recent app scans. When he read the number of the incoming call, he moved away from his desk before answering. Once out of earshot, he tapped the answer button and listened.

'It's time you came home.'
'Okay Mum. I'll come home straight away.'
Seeing Charlie at his desk, Adam approached, looking rather upset.
'What's up kid? You don't look so good.'
'Sorry, I just had some bad news and need to go home.'
Remembering the conversation with Mike, Charlie tried to look surprised as well as concerned and played out the charade as per Mike's instructions.

'Anything I can do?'

'Nah. I just need to go home. That was my Mum.'

'Well if I can be of help, just give me a call when you're ready. Anything I need to know before you go?'

Adam collected his thoughts before replying, he too playing the game as his fake Mum expected him to.

'Only, that I'm not sure when I'll be back. If you need any help ring this number and I'll get back to you as soon as I can, otherwise all is good. The app is secure and will remain so.'

In the short debrief Charlie, noticed the clinical precision in Adam's voice. It was the first time he'd thought of the kid as an ethical hacker after confirming his association with New Scotland Yard, and felt a new respect for his skills.

They shook hands and as per Mike's instructions. Charlie didn't make a fuss and wished him well, knowing they would never meet again. The brilliant young man closed the door quietly behind him. On the street and leaving his secret mission behind, he headed in the opposite direction to New Scotland Yard, taking a right turn, then left. He entered the Underground, taking a train to Westminster. Above ground, he phoned his commanding officer.

'I'm home, Mum,' hung up and waited.

A few minutes later an unmarked police car pulled up alongside him. The kerbside back door opened, and he got in.

'Welcome home son. Now, let's talk about T*he Party*!'

The Party was the code name given by Jo Daley to the final swoop on the current target, The Wolf. As they talked, Jo didn't mention her quarry by name or give any indication of who their person of interest might be. The car wove in and out of the traffic, just like any other London driver, keen to get around the city with minimum delay and stress.

After about an hour, they reached Paddington Station where Adam was dropped off. He was greeted at Platform 4 by two plain-clothes officers and all joined the train for Dorset, where the highly anticipated party would take place.

Chapter 37

Since Vasile arrived in Dorset a few days earlier, Anna had noticed that he seemed nervous, edgy, looking over his shoulder quite often. He wasn't his usual confident self but tried to hide it as best he could with stories of home, jokes and over-doing the comments on the beautiful Dorset landscapes as they talked and walked around parts of the countryside. Before long, Anna decided to confront him. As they were looking out over the Jurassic coastline, sipping their coffees, now was the time.

'I've noticed that you are not quite yourself, Vasile. Is there anything wrong?'

Her boyfriend hesitated, before replying.

'My love, I have done something bad, something very bad – something dangerous!'

Anna did not respond, hoping Vasile would fill the quiet time with an explanation.

'We are both in danger and, other than disappearing to another part of the world, I don't know what I, or we, can do about it.'

'What have you done this time?' she asked, not expecting much from him in response.

'You don't need to know. But for your safety and mine we should leave Dorset tonight and never return.'

'And go where, back to Romania?'

'We can't go home, and we cannot stay here. We must try to start a new life away from everything and anything to do with our past. And we must do it tonight under the cover of darkness.'

She reached out to hold his hand and saw the fear in his eyes.

'You know I will go wherever you go, but you must promise me one thing. You must promise to have a normal life, away from computers, tablets and smartphones. You must turn your back on your old way of life and be a normal guy. Do you promise?'

With the likelihood of a life-threatening confrontation with The Genie closing in on him, Vasile knew that his career as a hacker was over. He was washed up but chose not to mention the severity of the danger they were in. Instead he looked into Anna's eyes.

'I promise.'

To hear him say those two words was enough for Anna. It was what she had always wanted from him. His choice to live precariously was constantly on her mind. She did not want to be a part of her boyfriend's criminal activities and had waited patiently for such a day to arrive. She was happy and put to the back of her mind her earlier thoughts about what Vasile might have done. Tonight, they would leave for a new life, a normal life somewhere else in the world.

She noticed Vasile's mood shift as he noticed something out of the café window. A large, black SUV had pulled up by the cafe. Two men, looking almost local in their Barbour jackets, got out and headed towards the cafe. Vasile shifted nervously in his seat, then spoke.

'Quick! Pretend you do not know me. These men are coming to talk with me. I will sit over there and speak with them but promise you will not do anything to draw attention to yourself. Just act normal, drink your coffee and look at the view.'

Vasile quickly relocated to another table before the men entered the cafe. Immediately noticing him however, they approached and sat opposite. Addressing him in Russian, the conversation was short and to the point.

The Genie spoke first in a cool calm tone.

'Vasile my friend. We have known each other for a long time. You are one of our brothers on the Dark Web. We are family!'

Then the Terroriser followed with a hard, threatening intensity in his voice.

'You are no longer family. You turned on your brothers. Now you owe us!'

Vasile pleaded with them. He needed them to understand that he had been duped, and that his dark web actions were an accident and how he would never have done this on purpose. Once he realised his mistake, he told them, he'd removed the data file, hoping no harm had been done. His tone was entreatingly apologetic and was a plea for a mercy.

The Russians were not convinced. The smaller of the two, opened his jacket and slowly drew something from his inside pocket. It was an envelope, which he slid towards Vasile, nodding for him to open it. Inside were photographs of him and Anna, with a note that read,

£100,000 in 48 hours and we let you both live

Vasile was cornered. He protested the best he could, but soon conceded there was nothing he could do without risking Anna. His true love continued to look out the window, resisting the urge to glance towards the three men. Instead, she followed proceedings the best she could through the reflection in the glass, made easier by the dark, clouded skies.

Two more vehicles pulled into the car park. Further afield, Anna could see another car blocking the exit to the main road.

'Oh no!' she almost screamed.

'More Russians are coming! We're in trouble, we're in trouble!' she whimpered. Trying not to draw attention to herself, she went back to her silent observing.

Adam Barth monitored the situation from the car positioning carefully to block the exit to the main road. Jo Daley was in the second car. Ahead, the first car was positioned close to the café entrance. Anna could see all three from her position but Vasile and his two unwelcome companions appeared to be unaware that anything was happening in the car park.

Four people dressed casually in all-weather jackets, emerged from the first car. After scanning the area one of them passed a signal to Jo Daley's car. Jo jumped out, quickly striding up to join the four. Behind her followed three more guys, each with eyes darting around the area. They moved stealthily forward ready to react to any threat of danger.

The back entrance to the café was now covered by two additional officers. They emerged from some large grassy bushes and with no fuss and very little indication of who they were, the back door of the café was opened. Inside, the temporary staff, all special forces employees, readied themselves for the climax to *The Party*. All exits were now covered.

As the café's front door swung open, the two seated Russians shot quick glances over their shoulders, but it was too late for them to react. Vasile spotted his chance, and with a quick move, up-ended the table, sending his two oppressors crashing to the floor under furniture and menus. In a brief second, the small room filled with officers carrying hand guns, drawn and pointing towards the surprised men and Anna.

'Armed police stop! Don't move! Armed police! Don't move!'

Everyone froze!

In the mayhem, Vasile had managed to reach Anna to pull her away towards the kitchen door but they were blocked by a large man wearing a smart-arse smirk that said.

'Oh, no you don't!'

No-one moved except Commander Daley. She stepped forward once the scene was deemed to be under control by the frontline officers.

'Gentlemen and lady, you are now under arrest.'

She read them their rights. It was the perfect climax; No bullets! No blasts! And no fast cars!

'Take these two men away,' she said, pointing towards the Russians. Once their hands had been secured with plastic ties they were led away. Once out of sight she beckoned Vasile and Anna to sit down. They did so willingly, shocked and unaware of who they were facing.

'My name is Jo Daley, and I'm Head of Cyber Crime Unit at New Scotland Yard. Let's not mess about. You are Vasile Lupei, the well-known Romanian cyber-criminal, and you,' looking at his companion, 'are Anna Sala, currently working as a waitress in Dorchester. You are boyfriend and girlfriend, if I'm not mistaken?'

Jo paused to see if either Vasile or Anna would fill the quiet space.

Vasile was reluctant to give anything away that he didn't have to.

'You are correct about our names and our relationship but what was the term you used, *cyber-criminal?* I'm not so sure about that. What is a *cybercriminal?*'

Jo smiled, leaning forward to fix her eyes on Vasile.

'Well, Mr. Lupei, - or should I say, *The Wolf* - we've had you and your lovely girlfriend under surveillance for some time. We have amassed evidence that links you both to cyber–crime and crimes against the United Kingdom. I will happily list each one if you like. It's your choice. We can do this the hard way, or we can do it the harder way, or', she softened, 'we can discuss your options like adults. Which is it to be?'

Vasile looked at Anna. Her face said it all.

'Okay, you are correct. I am *The Wolf.*' Anna has played no part in my activities.'

'I'm not so sure about that. Under UK and International Law, your partner is an accessory and therefore as deeply involved in your activities as you are. You see, Mr. Lupei, by association she too can be charged.'

Vasile glanced over at Anna again, but this time ruefully.

'Okay, let's discuss our options', a deep sigh and puff out of Anna's cheeks confirming her agreement with Vasile's willingness to cooperate.

'Good! The right decision. Let's lay out your options.

Now very much in control of the likely outcome, Jo began to outline the choices.

'As I see it, you have only two options. Option One is to cooperate fully and maybe you and your girlfriend can come out of this situation with a fresh start somewhere outside of the UK. Or Option Two, is to not fully cooperate, and consequently be charged with offences under the Data Protection Act 1998, and the Computer Misuse Act 1990, which will see you both go to prison for a very long time.'

Never one for blind loyalty and always out to protect his own arse, Vasile replied.

'Not many options, not many at all.' He did not, could not look at Anna.

'Option One appears to be a good choice. What is it I can do for you?'

'Good choice indeed', acknowledged Jo. 'We will not discuss Option One here. Instead we will take you both to a secure and safe location and from there, my team will ask you both a few questions. The more you cooperate, the more our legal system is likely to look favourably on you both - it's that simple. Before you go, I have one more question.'

Jo fixed her eyes firmly on Vasile.

'And remember, the more you cooperate, the more accommodating we can be.'

Vasile and Anna nodded in agreement.

'We will cooperate with you as far as we can.'

Jo decided to push her luck. She had already hoodwinked Vasile and Anna into thinking there was a long list of charges against them for cybercrime. The truth was, that since landing in the UK, Vasile had only committed one relatively minor act of computer misuse. Anna had done nothing wrong. Jo was playing a bluff and so far, it seemed to be working, but she still needed an answer to her one big question.

'The two men you were talking with; from our surveillance we recognise them as cybercriminals. I need you to confirm their names?'

Vasile thought long and hard, looking up to the ceiling and down again.

'The shorter guy is called Ivan Stratski, or *Terroriser* and the taller guy, Vladimir Konseski, is *The Genie*'.

Keeping her face straight, the seasoned investigator gave no indication of her delight at receiving those names.

Bluffing a little further, she replied.

'Thank you. That was our understanding.'

She gave the order and Vasile was taken away for questioning in a windowless van. Jo saw it off from the café's entrance before making the call to Adam to come and collect her. After reversing a little to let all the other vehicles pass, he responded and pulled the car up, right outside the building. Once inside the car, his boss Jo couldn't contain herself any longer.

'Bloody hell! Bloody hell! Not only have we encouraged Vasile Lupei, *The Wolf*, to turn, but we've also apprehended two of the most active and dangerous cyber-criminals the world has ever had the misfortune to endure. What a day! What an incredible day!'

She couldn't help herself and threw her arms around Adam like any mother would do in celebration.

After all, it was Adam's ingenious use of the Sand Oil app that made it all possible.

After regaining her composure, she thanked Adam for everything he had done, adding, 'You stay here and make sure we haven't left anything behind, and besides I need your car to get back to London.'

'Yes ma'am, I understand.'

Marku, felt satisfied with the way he had worn his Adam Barth disguise, fitting in around the university and delivering the app security to the best of his considerable ability, but he was still trying to piece together what this sting was about. It was his first covert operation and it had seemingly gone well, but he didn't understand the details, and to be honest, he never expected to. Then it hit him. In her frantic celebration his boss let the name of the target slip – *The Wolf, Vasile Lupei*!

Unable to let it sink in he wandered aimlessly towards the cafe front door. He had been used and in the most terrible of ways. His sister's boyfriend, who she loved dearly, was now in the hands of the police authorities because of him. Dazed and confused by what had just happened a little practical reality dawned on him. Now wondering how he himself, was going to get home now, he figured he would just call a taxi and head over to Upwey, the nearest train station, and take it from there.

Not sure if he should or shouldn't do one final sweep of the café, he decided to step inside trying desperately to piece together the events of the past thirty minutes. He opened the café door.

Looking to the opening door, Anna cried out.

'Marku!', her tears quickly turning to joy as she raced forward to embrace her brother. 'Where have you been?'

Equally as shocked to find his sister here, the penny dropped with Marku almost immediately, and he shrugged his shoulders. They had all been used.

'You'll never believe me!' he said with an upbeat tone, now recovered from his confused state.

Righting an upturned table, Marku took his sister by the hand, guiding her to a chair. He then explained how he had been taken into custody, charged with offences against the UK and then released to the Cybercrime Unit at New Scotland Yard.

'But why are you here Marku?' Anna asked trying to find a connection between Marku and the recent rendezvous with Russians, Vasile and New Scotland Yard. Then it dawned on her.

'Marku! What have you done? You have led them to us and now Vasile has been arrested,' her mood quickly changing from short-lived joy to anger.

'My dear sister, I knew nothing of this! I didn't know we were tracking Vasile and you. If I had known this I would have preferred to go to jail instead. I'm so sorry I did not know!'

'I'm so confused Marku. One minute we are having coffee, then these Russians appear and soon after that, Vasile is arrested and taken away. And then, as if by magic, you appear!'

With emotions running high Marku didn't say anything more. He reached out and embraced her, repeatedly whispering sorry as they held each other tight.

After a few days of intensive questioning, Vasile was held on remand pending further investigations and a later appearance in court. Fearing the worst for Anna, he'd cooperated fully – he had no choice. Circling in his cell for something to do, he reflected on the events of the past few days. Deep inside he missed Anna - the love of his life. He concluded one thing for certain - his days as a dark disruptor and cyber-criminal were over.

The Wolf would pounce no more. The Wolf was dead!

Chapter 38

Lenny Tall arrived for work at the TechWatch TV Studio as usual but unexpectedly, his producer was stood by the front entrance with outstretched arms, ready to welcome him.

'Lenny, you're a genius! Last quarter's viewing figures hit one-point-two million on the first of May. That's more than one million for the first time in the TV studio's history. It's a great result.'

'Well I told you it would happen. I knew that one day the big exclusives would start coming to me,' Lenny replied, smugly.

While both men were busy congratulating each other, Lenny was tapped on the shoulder by a young lady.

'Mr. Tall! Mr. Cresswell would like to see you in his office immediately.' Lenny headed to the MD's office, smoothing his jacket and fixing his shirt as he went. He knocked the door, and stepped inside, not waiting for a response.

'Mr. Tall, please take a seat,' Cresswell directed. He was being quite formal, which was not the celebratory atmosphere Lenny had been anticipating. Cresswell began recapping on the past quarter.

'On the first of May, our flagship programme TechWatch, reached an unprecedented viewing figure. We've waited a long time for the elusive one million viewers on a single show, and you did it.

Actually, not just on one day but for several days thereafter.'

Lenny sensed that he and Cresswell were not alone in the room, so he glanced over his shoulder. Behind him, in the shadows, stood the studio's legal counsel, and their HR manager.

'You know Marc and Leanne, of course! I've invited them in for this momentous occasion,' affirmed Cresswell.

Lenny acknowledged Marc and Leanne, then turned back to face Derek. Maybe it was about his bonus? he thought.

Then came an uneasy pause as Derek made knowing eye contact with Marc, then Leanne before returning his full attention to Lenny Tall.

'Mr. Tall, you're fired, you piece of shit. You're fired!' What started with a calm assertive voice had now become a raging yell. 'Let me say that again. You're fired!'

Lenny could not believe what he was hearing.

'Just to be clear you mother fuckin', sonofabitch, you're fired!' Derek screamed, now one inch from Lenny's face.

'Mr. Cresswell, sir, I have no idea why you're saying this. No idea. What's happened? It wasn't me sir! Whatever it is it wasn't me.'

'Tell him Marc, tell this piece of shit exactly what he has done.'

Mr. Marc F. Thomas stepped forward, lifting a file from Cresswell's desk. From it, he pulled a document with a label saying 3D on the front.

'Lenny do you recognise this document?'

'Hmmm, ahhhhh, maybe, not so sure,' replied Lenny, starting to squirm.

'Take a closer look. It's got your name on it and you signed it in April.'

Lenny remembered.

'Sure, it's the 3D contract for the first of May exclusive; You know, the exclusive that got us to the 1.2 million viewers, remember?' he said, with more sarcasm than was wise. 'I sign these sorts of things all the time, you know that. I use my designated *Executive Powers* when it comes to exclusives.

'Did you read it?' asked the Legal Counsel, Thomas.

'Yeah, of course!' confirmed Lenny.

'How much of it did you read?'

'The first few pages and then I skimmed the rest. It's normal stuff.'

'Did you read the Schedule called 'Programme Timing and Frequency?' Thomas asked.

'No, I don't remember that one. Was it important?' asked Lenny.

'You dumb piece of shit!' spouted Derek. Leanne tried to calm Derek as he paced up and down the room.'

'Let me read it out to you, and for the benefit of everyone in the room. I'll leave out all the legal stuff and just quote the important parts.' Marc began to read.

> *Programme Timing and Frequency.*
> *Conditions: Broadcast Date is first of May.*

Broadcast script, as provided by 3D, is to be followed verbatim. Strictly no other broadcast relating to 3D to be made within 30 calendar days.

He then addressed the social media responsibilities.

Each social media broadcast starting at 06:30 should be made every thirty-minutes, as the main headline news. The social media broadcast must cease at 13:00 that same day and must not be repeated unless 3D gives written approval to do so.

Lenny started to wonder where this was going. The Legal Counsel continued.

On the same day, a special edition of TechWatch is to be broadcast covering the Sand Oil App and 3D. Strictly follow the storylines and script provided. Names and addresses of interviewees will be provided by 3D before 11am, the same day. Once completed, each interview is to be shared with 3D for review and selection, with the final selected interviews to be shown on the TechWatch broadcast where indicated in the script. Failure to comply with the above Conditions as outlined shall be deemed a serious breach of contract and result in appropriate action being taken against the TV

> *Studio, with Penalties outlined in Schedule 5 becoming due immediately.*

'Shall I get on to the *Penalties* in Schedule 5?' Marc asked the now-troubled TV programme anchor.

Lenny nodded reluctantly, not really wanting to hear anymore.

> *Schedule 5 – Penalties:*
>
> *Failure to comply with any of the above Conditions shall be deemed a serious breach of contract, the terms of which are here outlined:*
>
> *The lead anchor, Lenny Tall, shall have his employment terminated with immediate effect. The aforesaid TV Studio shall pay 3D the sum of £5,000,000 in damages with immediate effect.*

'Oh, and here's the best bit,' Marc said with a sarcastic eloquence.

> *To avoid paying the £5M in damages, each member of the Executive Team is to record a 60 seconds video apologising profusely to 3D for their broadcasting mistake and breach of contract. Each video is to be played live on TechWatch TV on a date to be agreed in writing by 3D.*

Having listened with increasing tension to every word spoken by his legal counsel, Derek Cresswell had to forcefully prevent himself from standing to applaud Marc's impressive and devastating performance.

'So Mr. piece-of-shit Tall, with all your fantastic broadcasting and negotiating skills, how do you propose we get out of this?' Derek moved in. Standing much closer again, his hot, angry breath blasting Lenny's face.

Lenny had to accept that he hadn't complied with conditions laid out in the contract. Social media posts had continued for days after the launch date, without seeking approval from 3D, and as each day passed the team had conducted street interviews and feedback surveys, all of which had gone out on the TechWatch programme with 3D's name all over it. Lenny Tall was oblivious to the fact that the contract with 3D had specifically forbidden such coverage. And he'd been oblivious to the clauses about interviewees. He chided himself for not having fully read the contract, but how was he to know that this one was so different to the usual sign-off papers? He realised that he had screwed up badly.

'Well, you know where the door is, now get out. We can at least comply with the first penalty clause and hope that we can seek some compromise on the rest.' Cresswell's order was final. 'Get out and close the door behind you!'

Lenny stood up, turned, and after trying unsuccessfully to muster a dignified exit, left the room. The door was closed behind him and Derek turned to his experts for guidance.

'We have no choice but to negotiate on points two and three, otherwise we're dead in the water. Perhaps there's a smart way out of this? Here's the telephone number for 3D. I'll call them now and set up a meeting.' Derek was keen to take control of the situation even if it did look dire. Within a few seconds, his call was answered.

'This is Derek Cresswell. I presume you know who I am and the company I represent?'

'Yes Mr. Cresswell. Yes indeed, I know who you are,' Mike confirmed.

'Mr. Day, you have my attention. You pretty much have the future of my company in your hands. I have already fired Lenny Tall, that useless piece-of-shit, replacing him as anchor with his far more professional, co-host, Lizzy Dawn.'

Mike had been expecting a call at some point from TechWatch, but Derek Cresswell had caught him off guard this morning. To give himself time to get his thoughts in order, he kept the chat light for a short while.

'That's good news Mr. Cresswell. I'm glad the infamous Lenny Tall has been released but I'm sure it won't be long before he'll be showing his ugly face again. God only knows why people don't see him for what he is – a two-bit liar and an arrogant creep who would sell his grandmother for personal gain. It's good he's gone. With Lizzy Dawn in his place I'm sure TechWatch will go from strength to strength.'

Derek Creswell wondered how talk of the future direction for his show tallied in with the threat of a heavy penalty leading to possible liquidation.

'Does this mean you will be releasing us from the £5m penalty for contact violation?' he asked with baited-breath.

'It's like this Derek; I have no intention of calling in either of the penalties or suing for damages. I like your weekly TechWatch programme but couldn't stomach it with that arsehole dishing out his nonsense. I want your TV Studio to prosper.'

'So, what is it that you do want?' Derek asked in a state of bafflement.

'Just a favour. And I want your word on it and I'll give you my word back that I will rip up that contract.'

'Okay I'm listening. What can I do for you?'

'There's this guy called Yeong Ji-Won, from South Korea. He's coming to London in the next few days. He's a genius. You will do yourself a big favour if you arrange for Lizzy Dawn to interview him live on national TV. His specialist subject is Smart City Management. I think Transport for London and the City Authorities would benefit from some of his insight. He's a great guy and his English is excellent.'

'It's a deal. You have my word. In fact, part of me is grateful to you for giving me a clear-cut reason for getting rid of that idiot, Tall.'

'It's my pleasure Derek. It was a long time coming but I've been holding a slight grudge against that arsehole since our school days together. Being the *arrogant prick,* he is, even to this day after all those years, this has been even more fun and worthwhile. It was my complete pleasure, but please understand that it was not my intention to cause you distress on the matter. And at last I can watch my favourite technology-based TV programme without having to see or listen to him.'

'That's very kind of you Mr Day. Will you do me a favour in return?'

'Sure.'

'Will you keep me up to date with of all your future tech' developments, so we can avoid situations like this in the future?'

'Favour granted. One final question before we can wrap this up like sensible guys. Tell me, where is Tall now?'

Derek was happy to answer, 'He was last seen being escorted off the premises with his tail between his legs. I'd swear he was crying as well.'

They both laughed. Lenny Tall had been fired and quite possibly reduced to tears, Derek Cresswell got to keep his TV company, Lizzy Dawn had rightfully been promoted to lead anchor, and Yeong Ji-Won had the perfect stage from which to communicate his vision for the capital called *Soul of the City of London*!

And Mike Day finally got his revenge on the school bully who made his early life so difficult.

Chapter 39

Following his recent very busy days, Mike was looking forward to some quieter time at home with just an occasional trip to the office to catch up with Charlie. After one such trip he was returning to his car. There was no sign of Lenny Tall. Mike smiled warmly happy Mr Tall would no longer be in his daily life. The flashbacks to their schooldays had stopped too. As he reached for the handle of his car door, he heard a voice behind him.

'Well Mr. Day, are you satisfied with what you have done?'

Mike turned around to listen to a familiar voice.

'Are you satisfied that you have destroyed the car insurance industry?' John Calcott glared. 'Are you able to live with yourself that tens of thousands of people have lost their jobs, possibly their houses and in some cases their families too?'

Mike stood tall, 'Well John, let's be specific about what we did. Sand Oil didn't destroy your industry. They disrupted it in the most catastrophic of ways. If anyone destroyed it, then it was people like you. You closed your eyes to the seemingly impossible and you got it wrong. At 3D, all we did was give Sand Oil and Gas the idea, and a very simple tool in the form of an £100,000 app to support the idea's implementation.'

'Nothing can save our industry now, it's all too late,' Calcott faded off, the loss in his eyes and a resigned anger still in his voice.

'It's not too late. You still have general insurance and other similar products to sell, but as you know, it is too late for car insurance. You can't win against the perfect synergy of a mega oil giant twinned with a radical new way of doing things that the public loves.' Mike paused. 'Here's a thought; the next time you're on your computer, Google *Gloria Stenson* and learn from this lady.

'And what else can we do?' Calcott asked, this time relaxing his face, blinking his eyes in the bright sunshine.

'Well John, that's easy,' Mike replied. 'Disrupt right back! And I'm glad you asked because I have an idea. Let's go talk about it over a coffee. Ever thought of becoming a utility?'

There was a smaller glimmer of hope for Insurance Direct. The resigned Calcott, out of shear arrogance and unpreparedness had dismissed the potential threat of digital technology. He knew it now and would never make the same mistake again. Over a coffee Mike explained his idea. The doom written on Calcott's face for weeks changed to hope. There was a way back after all. Mike Day, The Disruptor was right - *disrupt right back!*

Chapter 40

At the 3D office the next day Mike and Charlie were mulling around looking for things to do and Mike noticed Charlie didn't look happy.

'Why the glum face?'

'Well firstly you haven't told me about Phase 2 and 3, and secondly with all the recent excitement, I forgot about my bet with Lisa to cook dinner for us all. I'm not sure what to do or how to approach it. And to make matters worse, Jo's coming too.'

'Jo from New Scotland Yard, Head of the Cyber Crime Unit, that Jo?'

'Yeah! After she got her man, Mr. V, I think she called him, she came clean breaking her oath of secrecy. Her boss gave the okay in the end after Jo pleaded with him. Poor girl was worried about what I would do. After all she'd used me and sort of lied to me, as well as you and 3D!'

'Don't worry my friend. She was just doing her job and by all accounts we made a huge contribution. I'm not going to hold it against her, and neither should you. Besides Adam, assuming that was his real name, was great and I used Jo's name to defend our app against Calcott's final attempt to undermine our app by faking a hack.'

'I don't hold it against her,' smiled Charlie. 'We've already made up and that's why she's still coming to dinner tonight. And I haven't got a clue what to do.'

'Here's my advice. Keep it simple. An easy to prepare fish dish to start; no more than five ingredients for the main and a chocolate something for dessert. Yep chocolate, you can't go wrong with chocolate. And if you really feel like pushing the boat out then cheese with a fifteen-year-old tawny port to finish.'

'I was thinking home-made pizza and a Black Forest gateau from Iceland, made to look like my own.' Charlie was nodding, in agreement with himself.

'My friend, you've got to do something a bit more sophisticated than pizza and shit-flavoured plastic cake.'

'That's my problem. What?' He looked back at Mike with sorry dog eyes.

'I'm sure it will come to you. I promised Lisa I wouldn't meddle. She said that to fulfil the bet fully it had to be all your own work except when you needed to use kitchen equipment to aid you.'

'She did, did she?'

'Yep, all your own work, with no help from me.' Mike was smiling, almost laughing at the prospect of seeing Charlie trying to wriggle out of this one. Charlie repeated some of Mike's words. 'My own work. Kitchen equipment to help me.'

'Just so you know, Phase 2 has nothing to do with 3D – Sand Oil will bid for what's left of Insurance Direct. With the stock at almost junk level, it will be a bargain. Apparently, they want to leverage the claims handling experience even though there's a lot less these days. Better driving, lower speeds, better risk management in extreme weather conditions and therefore significantly fewer claims.'

'And Phase 3?'

'That's easy,' replied Mike. 'European rollout!'

'Wow!' exclaimed Charlie. 'Going big already!'

'Yep and by the way, nothing to do with Sand Oil just yet but our old friend Yeong Ji-Won is coming into town early next week for a live interview on TechWatch. Afterwards we're meeting him for dinner. He's been studying our app in conjunction with his Soul of the City vision and thinks there's an amazing cross-over for us to exploit. Something to do with healthcare or politics, I think. Social media too!'

Without any sort of response, Charlie's face lit up with a big happy expression beaming from ear to ear!

'See you later. I'm off to sort some stuff for tonight. Seven o'clock, wasn't it?'

'I think so. But you might want to arrive early so you can prepare.'

'Don't worry about that. Reckon I could be five minutes early.'

Mike shook his head from side to side. 'God only knows what crazy thoughts have just gone through that man's mind. One minute nothing, then a bit of advice from yours truly and the world, miraculously, is a better place.'

It was late afternoon when Mike left the office. Stepping outside, he could smell sweet lavender drifting on the light winds. It reminded him of the trip to Seoul. He thought of Charlie. Shook his head and headed for his car. This time no Lenny Tall nor John Calcott could be seen. He was looking forward to Charlie's dinner extravaganza, even if it was just a very crazy pizza.

That evening, Charlie was in control of dinner and had just served the first course.

'I'm so glad you all enjoyed the starter. I just decided to keep things simple.' Charlie briefly recalled Mike's advice.

The faint sound of the door-bell could just be heard. Charlie reacted first and got to his feet and was almost through the kitchen door and into the hallway before anyone else had worked out what was going on.

Curiosity filled the kitchen as the three dinner guests could hear muted chatter emanating from the other side of the dividing kitchen wall. As Charlie opened the front door, two young students pushed a large robot-like object into the hallway.

'We programmed it just as you asked,' they said.

'Did you test it also?'

'Sure.' The younger of the two Oriental-looking students replied knowing all too well that the programming took twice as long as expected and that testing was at best *lite*. In truth, neither really knew what Charlie was planning, so they did what they thought was best, and delivered the pre-programmed robot in time for the second course.

After thanking the two students and closing the door behind them, Charlie turned around, gathered his thoughts and pushed the object into the kitchen.

'And now, ladies and gentlemen, the main event! With the help of my assistant, C – A – T – E, which is pronounced as *Kate*, I will now prepare the most delicious, the most delightful and the most delectable main course you have ever had the pleasure to be served.'

The energy and enthusiasm from Charlie was captivating. Lisa and Jo edged closer, eager to inspect CATE, while Mike, bent forward with his head in his hands, trying to hide his embarrassment. Mike had met CATE before in the lab. He wasn't going to spoil the show. It was either going to be a major triumph or a complete disaster, but he didn't want his friend to lose out on his moment of glory, so he leaned back in his chair, removed his hands from his face and began to clap.

'Bravo Charlie. Bravo! What does CATE stand for?'

'Licking his lips with hungry anticipation, Charlie faced his audience and replied. CATE stands for Chef's Assistant to Everything.'

Mike continued 'Bravo Charlie. Bravo! But what does that actually mean?'

Lisa and Jo crept even closer, leaving their seats and slowly circling CATE, both simultaneously running their eyes up and down like scanning machines.

Charlie encouraged the women to have a good look. He was proud of CATE. It was several years in the making and now was the perfect opportunity to show what it could do. After circling for the third time, Jo and Lisa sat down again.

'To answer question from my esteemed colleague: CATE is a chef's assist. She can be operated using an app, a remote control or through a highly advanced voice recognition technology interface. See here.' Charlie pointed to two microphones protruding from CATE's ears.

'All I have to do is turn her on...'

'That might take a while!' shouted Mike. The girls laughed.

'All I have to do is switch her on', Charlie ignored them, 'and wait for CATE to wake up.

We can begin prepping and then cooking the main course. In exactly thirty minutes each one of you will be served a dish that's unique to you and to your exact requirements.'

The girls were enthralled. They'd never seen anything like CATE before and certainly not Charlie acting like circus ring showman in front of his big top audience.

'And now, ladies and gentlemen, we shall begin.'

'CATE! Ask Lisa what she would like for dinner.'

'Lisa, what would you like for dinner?' came a humanoid voice.

Lisa thought for a moment.

'I'd like fish and chips.' CATE didn't respond.

'Sorry Lisa. You must get CATE's attention first. Say her name, pause briefly and then say in a clear voice what you want for dinner.'

Lisa cleared her throat and tried again.

'CATE. I'd like fish and chips for dinner.'
'Thank you. I've taken your order for Flip Chips.'
'That's not a dinner, it's a circuit board!' despaired Charlie. With CATE not getting it quite right, there was a little giggle. Charlie pushed on.

'CATE! Ask Jo what she would like for dinner.' Jo was determined not to make the same mistake as Lisa. She wasn't going to make it so easy either.

'CATE. I'd like Toad in the Hole.' Nothing from CATE.

Charlie jumped in, 'A slight translation problem there'. He knew too well that the Far Eastern students had probably never heard of *Toad in the Hole,* and therefore didn't think to program it.

'That one's not in the recipe book Jo. Sorry. Try again.' Charlie urged.

'CATE. I'd like a Frog in a Pit for dinner.' Jo laughed, Lisa joined her, and Mike bellowed. Charlie looked annoyed.

Jo continued, 'No wait! CATE. I'd like Chicken Madras, with pilau rice, an onion bhaji, keema nan and saag aloo!'

'Now you're taking the bloody piss,' yelled Charlie. Everyone was bawling with laugher, except Charlie.

'Oh well, back to the drawing board,' he conceded. CATE was a disaster. The students had only programmed it with all the Asian food dishes they could remember.

It took several minutes for everyone to recompose themselves. Whilst Charlie sat in a heap of bewilderment, the girls wiped away their tears of laughter.

'My friend. I haven't laughed so much in ages, and as the appointed adjudicator in this bet, you've passed with flying colours. But let's hope robots don't take over in the kitchen anytime soon. Pizza anyone?'

He pulled out his phone, opened one of his favourite apps and began reading the special offers.

'Thank heavens for Domino's Pizza. Now who wants what?'

- End -

Author's Notes

I hope you enjoyed reading The Disruptor as much as I enjoyed writing it. As a final note, I wanted to spare a few words to reflect on some of the characters depicted in this book. Whilst it may be obvious to some why I included them, I thought I'd elaborate a bit more to explain some of my thinking.

Mike Day (The Disruptor) – The driving force behind the basic disruptive idea. Every digital disruption needs a Mike Day and a partner such Charlie Duke.

Lenny Tall – There is no place in business for bullies. There will always be people to are resistant to change, especially disruptive change. Don't leave them behind. Take them on the journey with you and learn to know when to stop wasting your time.

Gloria Stenson – The model business owner for delivering great customer service. She was on the brink of losing everything but did what any good business does – re-invent itself. Gloria went back to basics, found a niche in the market and stayed relevant to the needs of her customers.

Frank Delaney – The powerful businessman with a long list of corporate problems just crying out for something new and radical to help transform and save his company. For Frank, it was all about finding a way to leverage existing assets whilst acquiring new customers. Sand Oil and Gas had the perfect lever to disrupt the market. There are many more levers in the market.

John Calcott – This CEO closed his eyes to the threats of digital technology and the power behind a simple idea. I don't think he could have done anything to prevent the disruption, but he could have been wiser to the possibility, and perhaps taken out some insurance.

Vasile Lupei (Dark Disruptor) – He tried to disrupt the disruption by hacking into and exposing the app's weaknesses. It's one way to raise doubts about the integrity and security of an app. Data breaches can destroy an app regardless of how good it is.

Marku Sala – There is always room in the world for creative thinking and genius. We all need out-of-the-box thinkers. Luckily the Sand Oil App provided the perfect opportunity to do just that.

Anna Sala – the glue between Marku and Vasile that provided the story line for a perfect ending. A happy ending! And rightly, the Vasile Lupei's, of this world, do need to be held accountable for their dark disruptive ways.

Andrew Dodd – just a normal guy fed up paying a high price! He was just looking for a good deal and is just like the rest of us.

Peter Langley – strong business knowledge and data insight is essential for a well-executed disruption.

Yeong Ki-Won (Disruptor) – I have an interest in Smart Cities and wanted to bring another dynamic to this global topic, as well as threaten the long-term success of the app in this book. Disruptors need to remember that their idea is only as good as the next disruption. And of course, I firmly believe that the potential for exploiting big data is as rich as exploiting oil and gas.

Charlie Duke – Every good business idea needs a thinker (Mike) and a doer (Charlie). Without Charlie, Mike's idea would have never come to market.

Joanne Daley - Policing the dark web is becoming an increasingly difficult challenge. The irony in that statement is that it's the advancement of technology itself that's making it harder and harder. Distributed Leger Technology (DLT) not given any room in this book will increasingly be used by the Dark Web. As a technology it's also got potential for global disruption – I have a few ideas for such disruptions should anyone care to ask.

There you have it. The Disruptor is born. What will be his next disruption? I've planted a few thoughts in this book. Can you find them?

Ray Sherry

November 2019

www.ingramcontent.com/pod-product-compliance
Lightning Source LLC
LaVergne TN
LVHW040044080526
838202LV00045B/3485